T0162156

Other titles by João Gilberto Noll available
from Two Lines Press

Atlantic Hotel

Quiet Creature on the Corner

LORD

LORD

João Gilberto Noll

*Translated from Brazilian Portuguese
by Edgar Garbelotto*

TWO LINES
PRESS

Two Lines Press
582 Market Street, Suite 700, San Francisco, CA 94104
www.twolinespress.com

ISBN 978-1-931883-79-5

Cover design by Gabriele Wilson
Cover photo © Jeff Cottenden
Typeset by Sloane | Samuel
Printed in the United States of America

Library of Congress Cataloging-in-Publication Data
Names: Noll, João Gilberto, author. | Garbelotto, Edgar, translator.
Title: Lord / João Gilberto Noll ; translated by Edgar Garbelotto.
Other titles: Lorde. English
Description: San Francisco, CA : Two Lines Press, 2019.
Identifiers: LCCN 2018023930 | ISBN 9781931883795 (pbk.)
Subjects: LCSH: Acculturation--Fiction. | Brazil--Fiction. | Urban fiction.
Classification: LCC PQ9698.24.O44 L6713 2019 | DDC 869.3/42--dc23
LC record available at https://lccn.loc.gov/2018023930

1 3 5 7 9 10 8 6 4 2

This book was published with the support of the Ministry of
External Relations of Brazil in cooperation with the National Library Foundation / Ministry of Culture (obra publicada com apoio
do Ministério das Relações Exteriores do Brasil em cooperação
com a Fundação Biblioteca Nacional / Ministério da Cultura)
and by an award from the National Endowment for the Arts.

MINISTÉRIO DA CULTURA
Fundação BIBLIOTECA NACIONAL

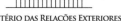

MINISTÉRIO DAS RELAÇÕES EXTERIORES

ART WORKS.
arts.gov

The secret interiors of these post-human fortresses solicit conspiracy, acts of sexual transgression. Illicit exchanges between dealers.

— Iain Sinclair, *London Orbital*

I exited customs pulling two heavy bags, a backpack hanging from my shoulder. I didn't even think of looking at the people behind the rail, waiting for arriving passengers. All of a sudden, I felt amazingly calm. If he didn't show up, I'd go to a cheap little hotel and return to Brazil the following day. I'd keep on walking down the hall, having those expectant shadows behind the rail by my side—those who always seem to have nothing else to do but wait sedentarily for the ones who don't stop moving, departing and arriving. I had arrived at Heathrow Airport in London. An Englishman had invited me for some kind of mission. Although he had sent me the tickets from Porto Alegre to São Paulo to London…I don't know, something was telling me he wouldn't come through. That it wouldn't matter if I called him at either of the numbers he gave me, one his office, the other his residence. That from that moment on those London numbers wouldn't belong to him anymore; maybe they didn't even exist in the city's listings. Walking down the endless hall that would certainly take me to the airport's exits and taxis, I knew ruminating about all of it was to pick at an open wound that needed to heal. I was in London now, for a special reason, the Englishman had invited me. But it seemed very unlikely that he'd show up at the airport or in any other part of that city in mid-winter—winter that I still hadn't felt inside that airport with its artificial climate, insulated from the world outside. He perhaps intended to take advantage of my gullibility with his invitation, though he didn't know that I don't suffer from gullibility per se. I'd tortured myself with doubts about the trip up to the day of my departure, mulling over the Englishman's intentions. Yes, the truth was I didn't have any choice. So I came. It seems easy to say, "So I came"—to be able and willing to suddenly cross the Atlantic, without having anything that needed my attention back home. But I can affirm this is one of the hardest things I've ever said in my not-so-short existence: "So I came." I could have made excuses. But no. All I had to do was to swap my loneliness in Porto Alegre for my loneliness in London, and I'd have a little extra money to support myself while in England. He'd promised me a mission—hadn't he?—a job like any other in principle, but I didn't know exactly what kind of job; any improbable task could be waiting for me, and I wanted to believe, walking down the airport's hall, I wanted to believe I was ready for him not to show up and to spend the night in a cheap room in Soho, perhaps, unable to stay one more single day outside Brazil—with only thirty pounds in my pocket and maybe not even that.

I could stay put on a bench at the airport, thinking perhaps that he would still come to pick me up. I had met him only once, in Rio, when he asked me to please send my books to his address in London because he couldn't find them in the bookstores he had visited that afternoon. He was returning to England the next day. He said he needed to understand something in my work—something that even I did not recognize but that had interested him for a number of years—he was writing a book about it. If I'm not mistaken, his book was about the senses. Was that it? Well, if not, I won't mention it again, I told myself as I dragged my bags toward an exit where he'd be waiting to tell me about my first assignment: where to go…where I'd be living…and maybe I'd never leave again, who knows?

I saw a public phone and a young woman selling phone cards behind a counter. I still had the crumpled piece of paper with his numbers in my shirt pocket. When I touched the startlingly cold receiver, I heard a voice behind me. I turned around as if I already knew who it was. The person whom I had started to not understand. I stood in front of him. I, who had lived all those years, let's say naked, in Brazil, without friends, barely making a living from my books, writing in short bursts, going through rough patches and doing all sorts of juggling to hide my material precariousness— hiding it for what exactly I don't know, since I saw almost nobody in Porto Alegre. Yes, during the interviews for the release of my last book, I put on an act: I am going to spend some time in London, representing Brazil…I'll do my best—the guffaw rising in my trachea but not coming out…do you understand?

We looked at each other. We said each other's names as if it were necessary to confirm we were present. To reassure ourselves. We clasped hands. His were cold, but not as much as the phone. It was cold in London, he said. It had snowed the day before.

He said we were on our way to the train station. He pointed me toward a large glass door. He said we'd go by train to the city center and take a taxi from there.

Where would we end up? I wanted to ask him. I knew deep down that he'd be in charge of everything up until a certain point, and whatever needed to be done would be—maybe not necessary to my benefit, but it would become evident that it was the most sensible thing to be done regardless of whether I could handle what was coming. The orders would come from him until I could…not dismiss him, no, never that…but hold on to some autonomy, which would always be limited…that I knew, too. After all, I was in a country I'd never been to before, and I lacked the youth that might make me easily adapt.

We looked at each other in the train station, bags at our feet; there was no one around. He said that we'd stop by his work. There was an empty office because his colleague was on vacation, and I could rest there until he took me to my new home in Hackney, north London. Hackney, I repeated in silence, as if the sonorous pronunciation would give me some kind of guarantee I still couldn't name. And what might I want any guarantee about? To be happier than I'd ever known happiness could be? To die late, after I'd become totally destroyed, or to take fewer and fewer risks until life became inoffensive? No, this man represented no danger to me. Neither did the city of London, which I was ready to take in. I didn't need any guarantees.

From the black hole to our left, I heard the ever more intense rumble of the train that would take us to the city center. The train was long, so it took a while for a car to come to a stop in front of us. We got on and put my bags on the luggage rack.

This man could be a companion in the numb center of my hopelessness, which I had long ago stopped waiting for. Why in fact did he call me in my hometown in southern Brazil? Why did he beg me to come to London on a mission that sounded so special?

Our breath escaping through our thick coats was the only thing that existed between us for a long part of the journey. An Englishman and a Brazilian, having so much to say, in principle, about the imminent arrival of one of them in that immense city. But now, on the train, all we felt was the barely discernable movement of two bodies living alone, without any surprises.

We're here, he said, and we had to pull the bags through another gigantic, crowded train station until we arrived at a taxi line. A black man was trying to organize the line with a placard or something in his hand. He said something I didn't understand, possibly in an accent from the Caribbean. My English companion said the man was telling us to go to the spot marked with a number one on a sign at the curb. We'd be next.

Was it cold? Not really. An inner voice whispered to me that if I ran along a wire fence following an airplane landing at a forgotten airport in Scotland or Ireland, if I ran—scratching my nails along the wire fence that separated the road from the runway—then yes, I'd feel real cold in my nostrils, but I wouldn't otherwise.

Side by side, my English companion and I were already seated in a typical London taxi, with ample space between our legs and the driver's cabin for our bags, which remained comfortably in view.

Where were we going again? Oh, to his work. I'd wait for an hour or two in the silent office of his vacationing colleague, the bags resting in the corner of the room. I needed to repeat it all to myself so nothing would escape me, no act, no chapter, so if I needed to testify to the authorities in the case that this Englishman—who even now looked like my benefactor—suddenly failed me, and yes, disappeared forever, even after saying he would take me to his office... Was he really going to open his life to a stranger? Anything could happen, maybe he was bluffing; I've seen it all in this world: people of all kinds, some of whom take revenge on entire nationalities, in this case Brazilians, because they never lack for a reason, always having one; I don't doubt that I could do the same if I were him; I would leave me alone in London, without the money (what he had called a fellowship) or any way to pay rent for the house in Hackney; I would leave me just like that, with offering my wrists to the first policeman to handcuff me, deport me…or even worse, never let me go.

But there we were, pulling my bags once again up the ramp behind a large building, three, four stories high, close to London's center, after we'd passed Buckingham Palace, St. James's, and so on, in the taxi. There we were, dragging my bags up the staircase, there was no elevator in the centuries-old building. It all seemed like a difficult stage we had to get through before another stage could begin.

He stopped in a narrow hall and showed me his name on an office door. I didn't read it. I was distracted looking at his ring. He turned and pointed me to the office where I'd wait for him, for an hour or so. We put the bags in the corner of the room. There was a table with chairs around it, as if people attended classes here, small lectures, meetings with a department head, etc. The walls were covered with books. I trailed my hand over them as if to confirm the reality I was living in. Though I knew I was not living an unreality per se—like those born out of a simple dream and ending up in a nightmare, which we can only escape from when we wake up sweaty, trembling, and confused.

I knew I would be alone in that room. I could sleep if I wanted to, or read a book—I passed my eyes over their spines, ascertaining that most were Portuguese editions about Portuguese subjects. I knew I'd have to justify to someone the reason for my presence in London someday, waiting for the Englishman to give me instructions as soon as he finished his meeting in an hour or so, even if the task for now was just to go to Hackney—that distant neighborhood in the north of London, full of Vietnamese and Turkish immigrants, outside of what the travel brochures usually showed on the city maps.

There was a gigantic volume on one of the shelves. I could barely hold it in my hands, still trembling from the weight of the luggage. The title was *Expansionism*. I was frightened to have picked it out from among all the other volumes. I don't know if it was because of its theme or its physical grandness, but it looked like it kept expanding moment by moment. I couldn't keep up with its weight, I must confess. I struggled to put it back in its place on the shelf. After all, what good would it do me to snoop around Portuguese Expansionism, a dead subject, when I had to prepare myself for the task that required so much more from me than I felt I could offer? Or would the task require nothing besides the fact of living in Hackney and keeping my name to a certain quality as a guarantee for a circle of English people to whom I still had no access?

Looking at it a different way, was I really representing Brazil? I had written my books, yes, but what could they possibly reveal that was not already familiar to anyone born and raised in the country I had just arrived in without knowing exactly what for?

Nobody knew the exact reasons a Frenchman chose to live in Scandinavia or a Russian dreamed about the vines of Chile. Who could know me? A deluded Brazilian who suddenly found himself surrounded by the Portuguese editions of a poet and scholar from Lisbon on vacation in the Algarve (it seemed), and whose name I couldn't remember because my mind had started to forget names. One could suspect that I was experiencing a sneak attack of amnesia, or becoming a victim of Alzheimer's.

But nobody here would suspect that they had brought a man to their country who had started to forget. They? Or only that one crazy Englishman, hatching a plan in the name of some institution where he only pretended he worked? Pretending to me and me alone because he had noticed I was already living in forgetfulness. Perhaps it would be better for his project if I died without ever knowing the name of this place, or even a simple thread I could follow to arrive at something that might make some sense to me.

Besides, had I been in any condition to decline his invitation? How would I be living back in Brazil in three, four months, if all my attempts to live beyond my books continued to fail? Yes, I was going through a dangerous bout of writer's block.

Yes, all that was left for me was to pose, ineffably, as the proprietor of the books I'd written, and to believe with conviction that they had gained some kind of prestige both inside and outside my country because of some translations. All that was left for me was to come here before I had to start screaming in vain for help.

Then the Englishman opened the door of the aforementioned Portuguese poet and scholar's office. I was asleep. I opened my eyes. I didn't recognize him at first. Was I home? Who was this blond man who had entered the room? A visitor of mine? For the first time he smiled openly.

For a moment, I wished I were home in Porto Alegre. I wished I didn't have to continue this journey, drag my bags God knows how much longer, to the farthest suburb in the city, enclave of the immigrants who were most deprived of those luxuries of the city's center that I saw out of the corners of my eyes as I was coming from Heathrow and talking to the Englishman, who was casually showing me some of the landscape, as I plated my role of attentive visitor.

The taxi drove along Old Street and then Hackney Road; more and more warehouses and factories filled the view. Then we arrived, finally, at my address on Mare Street. My apartment was on a corner, on the second floor above a Vietnamese restaurant. The restaurant's owner was the one renting the place in the name of the Englishman or his institution. I was going to live there.

An outside corridor behind the restaurant—completely dark in the early evening of a London winter—did not allow any door to be seen. It's here... The Englishman spoke with the knowledge of someone who had already visited the rooms I was about to inhabit. Oh, and there was a pallid moon under which purple clouds swiftly passed by as if in a rush to get somewhere.

Yes, I could see two locks. He showed me where the keyholes were. But he didn't take the keys from my hand. He let me try them myself since this would become my daily routine: open my apartment door in London, in a remote neighborhood, with tiny brick-walled houses to my right, each with a little garden in front. A long, unending street.

Every room had its corresponding cleaning supplies. In the hall that led to a staircase was a bucket with a blue liquid already prepared inside of it; a broom with rags was beside it. In the bathroom were rubber gloves, a big brush, and detergent to clean the bathtub, which looked immaculate, almost new. Same in the kitchen: more yellow gloves, sponges, and detergents on the counter. In the living room and bedroom: brooms.

It was time for me to thank him. After all, the first journey was concluded and I was in my new home, which I wouldn't have to pay for. If the Vietnamese landlord showed up at my door at the end of the month, I'd just have to say, "They're paying the rent, utilities, all of it," as if every stage of what I was living through in England wasn't just some sort of joke, which I wouldn't be able to solve except by offering myself to be handcuffed, without even a chance for deportation.

He said he'd like to show me the neighborhood. He opened a map and pointed to Victoria Park, not too far away. I could take my morning walks there like I used to take every morning by the Guaíba River in Porto Alegre, between the Usina do Gasômetro and the Pôr do Sol Theater. He knew

about my walks, but I didn't remember telling him,
if I even really had. He knew... I repeated silently.
He knew everything I had already forgotten about
myself. All I had lived until then seemed to be slip-
ping away. Only what I was experiencing in that
moment seemed to exist, the house I had to inhabit,
the new language. My old language, with which I
had been so intimate already seemed to be deserting
me—except of course the general notion of it, or
who knows, it might still provide me a little help
in some extreme case, like if I were about to die I
might still be able to pronounce a dear old word
from my childhood, one of those words you don't
even know you have inside of you until it comes out
when all the useless words of now drift away to the
point where the hard edge of that sharp longing can
reemerge in but one or two syllables.

We walked through the night on Mare Street
in that windy, cold neighborhood of Hackney, passing through its population of Africans, Caribbeans,
Vietnamese, Turks; he wanted to show me Victoria
Park, which he didn't know. Meanwhile, he pointed
to several Asian restaurants with cybercafés, in case

I needed them, since there was no landline in the house with which to connect to the internet; later, when I got back home, alone, I also saw that there was no mirror—over the following three, four days, I went after one; I found it at a beauty supply store—one of those oval mirrors with a handle to hold on to.

We were walking in darkness along a path of beautiful, elegant houses in front of Victoria Park. Suddenly, the houses' façades changed. They had iron bars on their balconies; they were hard, unfriendly. He told me that the architectural change was the result of the reconstruction after the bombings. Ah, I'm in the city of Churchill and his cigar, I murmured, I should not forget; I should do a memory exercise, who knows, something like recapping the historical facts from World War II onward in my mind. This might help me avoid embarrassing myself in front of people when caught in an unwise conversation.

Not that I was a complete idiot and couldn't remember anything—otherwise I wouldn't be in one of the world's capitals, having been called by an Englishman who belonged to an institution where there was a respectable library devoted to the Portuguese world, with that massive compendium on Portuguese expansionism; and when we were leaving, later, we passed a vast cafeteria where students laughed loudly and seemed to be having a really good time, as if that ancient building still contained the energy of the masses and retained it inside a mysterious womb, which now also seemed to want the strange presence of a Brazilian who wrote books that were mostly well received by critics but not by the public.

We approached one of the grand gates of Victoria Park, and I could imagine myself running along one of its promenades on a foggy morning and stumbling over a homeless man asking me for coins to maybe restore his pride for a few minutes. I held on to the gate's iron bars to make myself firm, abandoning any imminence of thought, of sensation, focusing only on an indistinct vision of the park at night, even though it was not six o'clock yet. He said: It's closed.

That's when I thought: that I wouldn't want to

be in any other place but here. Or, at least, there
was no better choice. What would I be doing in
Brazil? Staring at the February sun, blinding myself
in peace? I needed to be here, though I lacked any
hint of passion for it. I imagined the park's daytime
splendor, even in winter with the branches dry and
all that, yes, everything could be beautiful in this
hemisphere of shadows if one knew how to look. I
should have imagined this world back when I used
to dream of a life outside the tropical realm to calm
my melancholic adolescence; now, although I felt I
was in the right place, and lucky to be here under
the (for me still hypothetical) shelter of an institution and a blond Englishman I should trust, I was
unable to summon the necessary enthusiasm to live
in this frozen world of the North.

Some branches were so thin that they fluttered
in the wind. I held on to the iron bars of the gates
to Victoria Park with redoubled relief. I would not
leave this place until it was proved to me a better
one existed. I was sure I wouldn't be given a second
chance. This sureness was tested by a chilling cold.
I was freezing. Deep down I couldn't see how this

opportunity could improve my life—which I still hadn't learned to imagine, much less ask for.

I glanced at the Englishman and loosened my grip on the iron bars of the park gates. I knew that, for good or bad, uncertain or not, he calmed me down. A sincerity, which I didn't want to admit existed, seemed to emanate from his core. But to blindly believe in someone from a foreign country would not be a good idea, at least not until things were clear: a solid document, an invitation letter with a stamp from the organization—if they used stamps here to prove the authenticity of institutions or whatever it was he was representing.

He smiled vaguely. Perhaps because he was showing me a better side of Hackney. Over there, there were no abandoned warehouses or smells of grease coming from the Vietnamese restaurants. And I had no more longing. No desire for anything new to arise along with the new morning. What I had was enough. And that little, almost nothing, could make me indifferent to everything else.

Or did I have a lot? Did I have it all? If it were up to me, I could just go back, back to the house, which

I now wanted to call my own, although I still was not sure he would pay—through his institution— my rent each month. If it were up to me, I could go back to sleep, try the bed I'd been given, its blanket and pillows. If it were up to me, I would solve all my dilemmas with some good sleep. And I would not wake up until the late winter brightness broke through the curtainless bedroom window through which I could see bars and debris and a small tree with bare branches far from budding. If it were up to me, I could die for the next few hours; not want to know the legitimacy of the Englishman's intentions: He who had called me from a distant country and seemed to want to extract some unsullied realness from me—as if I were ready, coming from the authenticity of a southern land, as if I could provide the British with a type of unparalleled loyalty unheard of among other peoples. Me, huh? I muttered and looked at my shoes, already muddy from the London damp.

When I got home, the temperature inside was perfect. He had provided: I had seen him adjusting the thermostat before he took me to Victoria Park.

I wandered around the apartment, starting with the bathroom, where I looked for the mirror. There wasn't one. Vietnamese people were opposed to the act of looking at themselves, was it possibly that? My search had a purpose: I wanted to see myself after the voyage; see if I was still the same, if this person who had appropriated a house in the suburbs of London had been rejuvenated by the move; see if his skin was oily or dry or marked with wrinkles that would stop him from wanting to give up on his journey—for example, if he said no, he would be returning to Brazil on the first plane, or that they should expect no other decision from him except for him to wander around Europe until his legs no longer allowed, until he reached a point when everything flowed into infinity.

I lay in bed with my clothes and shoes still on. It was very comfortable. What would it be like to dream in that curtainless room that offered me a leafless tree, iron bars, and the debris that was once perhaps the immediate result of the Industrial Revolution? Would I dream of squalid nature or gears crushing me? From the pitched roof of the

Vietnamese restaurant below my window someone could come, break my window, and enter the apartment. I didn't believe anyone in the neighborhood would do me any harm. Who would see in me anything other than the so-called peaceful citizen, with nothing worth stealing?

Everything was peaceful. I didn't have to believe or stop believing. If I could sleep that night—and after the weariness of the trip, everything indicated that I would—if I could have that type of sleep that makes us brand new, I would venture into London the next day, even at my age. And in the afternoon, I would wait for the Englishman to call me on my cheap cellphone to advise me of my next steps. Where had I been all day? Looking for a mirror, because I need evidence that I'm still the same, that another has not taken my place. If this position doesn't work out for me, if everything I have lived up until now is nothing more than a mistake, I assume the Brazilian Embassy will be able to take stock of my dilemma and give me a return ticket to Brazil. The right, effective, translucent man will be the one to appear in that mirror I haven't yet looked into.

I rode home on the red double-decker bus, on the upper deck of course, holding the wrapped mirror I'd purchased. I pondered the difficulty I would have at home, looking at myself without disdain. Oval, with yellow edges, a handle to hold. A proper mirror from a beauty salon. Yes, I bought it at a store that specialized in beauty products. Full of Thai people, who seemed to find it amusing that I was there; me, this placid man as I said I am, stripped of his vanity and ignorant of his own features. They laughed, and I couldn't help but find it amusing too, as I chose the color and shape of the mirror. When I paid, I remembered how the Englishman had handed me the first installment of my stipend the night before. The money was inside a tightly sealed envelope and I didn't bother to count it. I trusted him, I trusted him so much that I preferred at times to silence my thoughts in favor of this confidence. Yes, I chose to deflect my doubt and evaluate him with obliquity. When the Thai woman gave me my change in coins of various sizes and shapes, and with numbers I could not quantify at first glance, I realized that I would have to get used to this country quickly, that managing things would soon be part of what they expected of me—what all these other people who were backing up the Englishman expected.

I found a nail on the wall above the bathtub where I could hang up the mirror. I would have to stand in the tub to see who this man was. Without taking off my coat or cap, I looked. I was an old man. Before, there had been no doubt that I'd reached a certain age. But now I didn't recognize myself, too much time had passed. What could they want with a man who could do so little? Or did they expect me to have the decanted wisdom of an old man? And what kind of wisdom could I possibly offer at a seminar, for example, or even at a small conference about whatever it was I still had left in me... my delirium? I rubbed my face with my hands as if to clean away the accumulation of time. Oh, I think I was experiencing extreme fatigue, my sight was hurting me—seeing the nakedness of my own face.

It was still day; I left home. I caught the 55 bus on Mare Street toward Oxford Street, where I had been that morning. I walked through the crowd, crossed Soho searching for a pharmacy, went to

Piccadilly Circus. There I found a store. I needed to shake my fear of going in and asking for some kind of product that would soften my wrinkles, the deep marks between the land of my nostrils and the tips of my lips. I was living in another country now, at last, and couldn't care less if they mocked me. Next time, I would go to a different store. I could not forget their blasé reaction to my appearance. I felt something very determined within me: I did not miss what I'd left in Brazil or anything in any zone of any country. For the time being, or perhaps forever, I would have to accept what they gave me here in London as the possible solution to continue my existence, the old man that I was, but not so old as to be unable to walk with some dexterity, nevertheless feeling very forgetful, with nothing to give beyond what I had already given: kindness, a diplomatic smile, my only contributions in this foreign land. Yes, I was depending on them, and some inner voice was telling me not to stray from that dependence. I would leave my bank account in Brazil completely empty. In fact, I had to go into that pharmacy in Piccadilly Circus and buy something that would transform me. Not into a young man, I wouldn't say that, but a man with an exemplary appearance. Or something like that.

I bought a face powder that came in a round compact. The saleswoman helped me find one to match my skin tone. She seemed convinced of her choice. I tried not to look in the mirror over the counter. I preferred to trust her competence as a cosmetics saleswoman. When I was about to pay, I noticed that this transaction involved many coins, a huge number of them. I realized that I still didn't understand them. I was illiterate when it came to the currency. So, I took some paper money out of my pocket and showed it to the woman at the cash register, let her take the necessary amount herself. And I left, putting the compact in my pocket.

It was starting to get dark. I went walking toward what signs indicated to be Trafalgar Square. I caught a glimpse of the National Gallery building and thought I would go inside. To my grateful surprise the admission was free. Instead of looking at the paintings—though I knew I passed close by a Raphael—I went looking for a bathroom. I peed.

The vast empty bathroom. In front of the mirror I realized that what I expected to see was not there. I took the compact out of my pocket, took it out of its box, opened it, and slowly rubbed the powder over my cheeks and forehead. If anyone saw me, they would certainly think of some artistic performance. I was a self-effacing person, I would do anything if this so-called world would continue sheltering me with some comfort, even if only a little, nearly none. Brazil was a fresco in the vault of my mind, but it didn't hurt me at all, I almost didn't have the sight to see it clearly anymore. To tell the truth, my mind had been deteriorating for a long time, it could barely sustain any memories. That's why I was applying makeup in the bathroom of the National Gallery, without anyone coming in or out, as if I were in my dressing room preparing myself for the party. I would be a distinguished man, with the soft skin of a gentleman. Everyone would hear me in the crowded auditorium. What was left for me to say after saying so much for so many years? What have I really said? I know I was applying my makeup perfectly.

I left the bathroom stiffer than ever. No one else

would ever recognize me again; I had transformed myself into someone who even I was seriously beginning to find strange. I immediately noticed a huge Murillo painting of Christ healing the paralyzed—he lay among a few men stretched out on the ground, suffering. Was there any way out but to heal the paralyzed? I wondered, feeling the weariness of having walked around London too much that day. I needed to attach myself blindly to the Englishman who had called me to London; I needed to reinvent him within me, allowing me to lose myself; I needed to allow the other to be born inside me, inside this very person whom I used to call "I," but who seemed so dissolved lately, ready and willing to receive the crude essence of the Englishman. I needed to continue my transformation so as to know how to proceed. I would learn how to shape this substance, I knew I would: to become the other and then another and then another.

I had come to London to become many—I needed to understand that once and for all. To be only one person was not enough for me now—like the single being I had been in Brazil... I was ready, yes, and so I had to go back to my apartment, earn my routine, deserve it.

I walked through the dark streets with slow steps, until I found the bus stop of the only city bus I knew of that could get me anywhere: my house on Mare Street in Hackney. It was a long walk to Oxford Street, where the 55 came and went, but I didn't need to know of any other means of transportation, other routes. When I'd gotten down to Oxford I could walk to countless places in the city, no matter how far they were; I was a bull on feet and human legs—just knowing that after anything, I could find my way back to Oxford Street, take the 55, and forty-five to fifty minutes later, depending on traffic, I would be under the blankets, listening to some classical music from one of the two FM stations I had found for that kind of music.

That evening, once inside the house, I went straight to the mirror. I didn't look as old anymore. If I dyed my hair a light brown... What I felt, looking at myself in the mirror, was not what one usually feels for oneself: there was no special attachment to this figure, perhaps just some distant sympathy like one feels for a relative they haven't seen in a long time, but with whom intimacy was exchanged during childhood. Someone with whom we can co-exist for a few minutes without solemnity or misfortune, but whom we can also quickly leave behind in search of another identity, the one that insists on escaping us. I was a dandy, I now understood very well, and no city in the world would suit me as well as the one I happened to be in at that moment. That was my fate from that point forward, and I needed to do whatever was necessary to continue pursuing it until the end…which would be near, I thought, returning the mirror to the nail above the bathtub. A dandy in Hackney, I thought and coughed.

In the apartment, I ate a bunch of grapes, a banana, fruit that had been waiting for me in the refrigerator. Then I swept the rooms though they had not a speck of dust. Then I took my tranquilizer to sleep since nothing new happened. What new events could possibly happen to me? The Englishman, always the Englishman, calling, showing up suddenly, knocking on the door, requesting my services. Or saying that the contract was terminated, because I didn't know how to take advantage of the opportunity I was given. I would ask him to take me for a lecture, just one, so I could show him and the whole audience how up-to-date I was on Brazilian trends— which was a lie, of course, I no longer remembered where I had come from. At that point, Brazil was just an insinuation, a pure abstraction to me. What I really knew was my way from Oxford Street to Mare Street, discovered paths from Oxford Circus, how to get to Piccadilly, to Trafalgar Square, to go on, to want more, more from the same place, in this city I had been summoned to. Yes, I wanted more; I clung to that invitation, which I would not decline easily, if he wished to know. Did he want me to talk about Brazil to an audience of six hundred people? Ah, a lake was coming for me, and I was getting in it slowly, very slowly, because the water was cold and I didn't have enough flesh yet to bear it. My skin, shivering leather. I looked around and saw no one. A hill over there. A horse grazing. More? To resist the sting of the ice on my skin and then drown myself in the lake. It should be easy for such a slim body. But I gradually understood that it wasn't. I got out of the lake; I reached the bank feeling almost autistic as had become usual, but I got out, I didn't drown. I was what? Six, seven years old. So, today, I found myself waiting for the Englishman. It was necessary for me to get involved. To break the shackles of that waiting and get involved: if I felt the onset of amnesia, I would need to recollect that and other images from my entrails, whether lived through or not, and from them I could extract—as one squeezes an orange, bit by bit, with force, with the difficulty exposed, worth points—I would extract from these images…what exactly? Laughter, because I didn't know of anything else; oh, yes, it was Brazil that I needed to talk about, this Brazil that I had just become unacquainted with and which I now share with you, ladies and gentlemen. The audience was drowning in laughter, I made their afternoon, if not their next day and beyond. My eyes watered, not out of emotion: the makeup was getting in my eyes and irritated them to the point that they seemed to cry along with all the outpouring around me.

Wiping my eyes with a handkerchief, I apologized, looking primarily at my English benefactor by my side. I apologized again, this time to the whole audience (I realized there were many young people among them) and I slowly walked out of the auditorium. I walked the streets with a mixture of shame and the pride of duty accomplished. I had said things to the public that I might use again in future lectures. Perhaps everything was just simple repetition, which people vehemently accepted because I knew how to stun them with my poetic rhetoric. The problem this time—if there was really a problem besides my not knowing how to renew myself—was that I didn't remember anymore. What I knew was that I was here in England, in its capital, having been called upon by an Englishman who seemed to need my services badly enough that without them his own endeavors could not progress. This I would never forget, because I still had the hope that if I carefully guarded the nucleus around which my story formed at that moment, I might one day recover the memory of what sustained that nucleus, its entanglements and consequences, its rhymes even.

I walked by a unisex beauty salon and decided

to go in. The girl offered me a magazine. I was pondering the light brown color I wanted for my thinning hair: a few tufts here and there topped with a bald spot. I sat down and the Malaysian hairdresser asked me if I wanted a short cut. I said I needed to color my hair. And I pointed to the picture of a young man on the wall. He had the hair color I dreamed about.

I could take the barber's cape from around my neck and get out of there, give up on the idea of making myself more artificial. But no, I repeated to her: That's the tone I want, please…

The dye trickled down my temples and mixed with my makeup, making a damned mess. The dye continued to trickle; crusts of foundation crumbled from my face, falling onto the fabric she had put on me for protection. Was it humiliating? I didn't know the meaning of that word anymore. Things no longer offended me enough. Protecting my self-esteem was no longer necessary because I had serious suspicions that I was no longer the same man inside.

Now I could see. I was a light brown-haired fellow, just like that handsome young man on the wall, and I was so rejuvenated that I felt I had been fully absolved at last for any damage I might have caused. I looked like so many men walking the streets of London—I could pass as one of them. My lack of definition was already greater than me, although I had lost myself and begun to suspect that even my English boss couldn't do anything to bring me back to me. I needed to keep up this task of being everyone somehow, because without it I wouldn't even make it as far as the corner: without asking anyone, I happened to have overcome being the individual whom I had mechanically created for other people. I had to find a new source for my new formation, even now in my fifties, and that fountain would come from him, that light brown-haired man with makeup on, who lived in London for the time being without exactly remembering why.

The crowd on the street sported that unrestrained energy people have when they leave the office, unless the London winter's early darkness was deceiving me and it was not yet time for their workdays to be over. Suggestible or not, I walked with more agility in their midst, listening to bits of stories, foolishnesses, quiet aspirations, confessions that my ears aborted in my eagerness to keep walking in the same direction. If I could be this man who pulsed stronger inside me, I would try with all my strength to stay here in London; now, yes, and I would write another story—I would publish in English the transformation of myself into an alien, but the transformation that would end up being morbid if I didn't steer it along a straight course. I would live in Bloomsbury. The very man who had summoned me to London would not recognize me, and I would lose all ties to him. I would become one of those immigrant authors without a precise nationality, without a flag to unfurl at their lectures or conferences. Everything was melting in my head, like the hair color and makeup trickling down my pathetic face in the mirror. I felt that my steps were more graceful now, in strange unison with the swift rhythm of the crowd.

Oh, I was mistaken again. The fact was that I was losing direction. I rambled along until I reached the banks of the Thames, my first sighting of it. There were not many people along its edges, and the cold froze me to the bone. I had already become a person who a police officer might find sleeping frozen in the streets; a man who, when responding to the questions of some authorities, would have no documents, language, or memory. Punished in a solitary cell for years and years. Or, rather, released without any trouble by a young, inexperienced policeman on his first rounds, and from whom would pour rays of sympathy for this heap of flesh without a name, destiny, or home.

Although today I was closer to becoming that man than ever before—I only had the slight guarantee that I wouldn't fall to the gutter of the Englishman sparsely financing me—a gentleman was simultaneously rising inside me, certainly the dandy I had never succeeded in becoming in Brazil. Yes, I was suffering from deep amnesia, especially about certain occasions, but I hadn't forgotten that this new gentleman had the wits of the boy who had walked into the cold lake, thus he wouldn't drown despite the shadow clouding his mind. I would not drown either. I would rise as another, whole and triumphant. I didn't care that people on the sidewalk

didn't notice me, that to them I blended with everything else: it was from being separate from the
crowd that I was constructing my new face, my new
memories. For now, yes, I was nobody. But soon I
would approach everyone with my new face and a
story I could tell from the first verse. Yes, it would
be written in verses, and I would recite them for my
new audiences.

The Englishman knocked on my door the next
morning. I woke up. He told me not to worry, and
that he would take me to the hospital to see if everything was all right. I asked for a moment to change
clothes. We took the 55 and got off at Bloomsbury.
I could hear our steps; the silence was brutal. We
passed a sign for the British Museum. I wanted to
make a comment, for example, that Rimbaud used
to visit the Museum's library. My voice didn't come
out because I was sure that anything I said would
sound alien—the man at my side was worried and
he couldn't hide it.

I filled out a form at reception. We entered the
medical unit. The Englishman looked like a hospital
employee, such was his ease in the halls. He asked

me to sit on a vacant bed. I sat down. Someone who appeared to be a doctor arrived. He began to examine me. "Yeah," he said with some harshness, then he asked me to lie down. He called a nurse. She handed him some instruments. And the doctor stuck a needle in my vein. I can't remember feeling such bliss in my whole life. The medication flowing into me had the numbing effect of pulling me out of the air. For the next few hours I wouldn't have to do anything to try and create continuity with things. What's more, I would have no fear of my destiny from that moment forward, which would be expected, boring, as it is in any patient under medical care in the ward of any hospital. I didn't believe anything worse could happen…this was it! I trusted, on the contrary, that during my stay the man throbbing inside me, whom I still didn't know, would have better conditions under which to come out. That when I awoke from the anesthetic, I would start living within another hypothesis of myself, and that I would work on it in secret, without my English friend noticing any change in my character or on the surfaces of my body. They had me hospitalized for some reason I didn't understand. I would use it to be born.

I died during the time I was sedated. When I woke up, I saw a nurse with an unfriendly face. She just said everything was fine and I could go. They had identified something about my health. I asked what kind of exam they had done. She didn't understand me, or she preferred to stay quiet. I left the hospital, out into Bloomsbury Square. That was the neighborhood I would want to live in...there, where they had doused me in it for a period of time I couldn't figure, perhaps to verify whether I had any signs of a health problem that might keep me from fulfilling my obligations to their official program. Or was the program less than official, just a byproduct of minds with some shadow power? I was involved in the plot of some lowbrow spy novel, and was now inoculated with some substance that would make me even more submissive—I, especially because of my clouded mind, would give them the key to discovering whatever it was I could not foresee. I was the fool of a global citadel. I would serve them in some task whose meaning I couldn't understand. But I was not going to cry or feel regret. And taking

JOÃO GILBERTO NOLL

a plane back to Brazil was out of the question.

The vein where they had stuck in the needle was sore when I folded my arm. I was on a corner, wondering what to do. If I went back home to Hackney, would it still be mine? Would the key I had still open the door? The wind cut into my neck; I raised my collar. If I called the Englishman it'd just go to his damned voicemail. In my mind, I had always belonged to London, there was no other city, no other country. When I returned to that lone image from my childhood in Brazil, I used my own hands to finish drowning that child who was always counting the days until he drowned. My childhood had been in these very streets where I now shivered with cold. Adolescence, youth, adulthood, always here. Not that I had a special love for all this that was always the same. It rained and I drooled. I could not contain the saliva in my mouth, perhaps because of some side effect of the procedure to which I was subjected at the hospital. I was like a child who didn't have the strength to express himself, drooling. If I felt hungry, cold, thirsty, in pain, none of that required me to bare myself to another person, because in this country I only had the Englishman to expose myself to, and I now had serious doubts he was still available to me. Maybe I was very sick and they no longer had any use for me. Who knows. But that hypothesis seemed a little remote to me now.

That's when I walked into the British Museum. Tourists from all over. I went to the Egyptian exhibit. I admired their distant gods. And I was enchanted by the smallest image in the museum, tiny: Apis, the god who was a bull. Exactly what I was for all those English people who wanted to make me sick. Yes, I was now seeing myself in a true mirror, and they would not mess with me. I didn't need mirrors in public bathrooms anymore, or even my own mirror at home; I was Apis, I could walk all over London if I felt like it—through every alley, through the parks, and I could even fast, like they no longer knew how to do.

What if I went to a pub then? Not to get a drink or to eat something, though I hadn't put anything in my mouth for days, besides one or two glasses of water to keep the bull standing. I went into a pub called The Bloomsbury. Let others look at me, let them see the other person within me. Perhaps the fact that I didn't drink or eat but just stood there staring at nothing might call somebody's attention to me. The waiter would come, I'd say I just wanted to rest, I just left the hospital and need to rest. Okay, maybe order some mineral water so the waiter will leave me alone. But I would stand there, not wanting to sit down. That would kindle the curiosity of one or another of the pub's patrons. That's what I needed in London. The attention of someone other than the Englishman who had been missing for I don't know how many days now as I had lain unconscious for that undetermined amount of time at the hospital. A drunk came up to speak with me. He complained about his wife. I took sips of my mineral water as if to savor the voice that addressed me, even if he did not distinguish me from anybody else... after all, he was a drunk. I felt his alcoholic breath as if it were the only shower I felt like taking. I didn't interrupt his speech, expressed no opinion, though I thought his wife was a lost cause. The atmosphere gave me the impression of a medieval tavern: a sourness in the air, bodies smelling badly, especially mine, which hadn't changed its clothes in a long time. Everything itched, my genitals, my chest, my scalp that still stubbornly burned by the dye. Oh, I had forgotten to check my appearance in the mirror, to see if I were still the man who had already changed so much, if I had already become someone else completely or if the hospital had at last been able to reconstitute the old features I'd left behind in Brazil. Where had I lost the power of recollection? I was only concerned with what I had gotten myself into, the city of London in winter, and in that moment, in the pub with the drunkard telling me about the extramarital achievements of his youth, then his daughter suddenly dead in the arms of his crying wife; a convulsion made him grab my neck as if he were going to strangle me, his fingers tightening on my jugular, suddenly my heart in flames—I drop the glass of water, it breaks, everyone looks—this is my only reaction; I am saved, hopelessly saved again.

Saved and drooling. Maybe this uncontrolled slobbering doesn't offer a solution. Yes, now I'm being watched by everyone in the pub, as I had hoped. Not because I knocked the glass over and was about to be strangled. But because I'm slobbering and still have the nerve to frequent a pub. I might ask: What makes me a man with such a lack of civic decorum for an evening drinking with friends? I could ask, but I don't, for one reason: none of this will matter tomorrow, when I'll be living the life of that man who is still lying in the hospital bed in Bloomsbury—that man stayed there while I was able to escape, thanks to the nurse's bad intentions. There lies a petrified version of me, with no desire to control the world or what belongs to it, a waiting stone. I will return in the dead of night; I will lift the sheet and lie down. And when the Englishman returns, he will see that the experiment was successful. I'll be that other one, ready to lecture in public squares about the issues that concern his fellow scholars, who still insist on hiding themselves.

But let's leave him there, in his well-deserved sleep at the hospital. The one slobbering here will try to find his house in Hackney. I take the 55—what would I do without this bus? I don't need to force the lock. The key opens the door easily. The apartment is still mine. Fruit in the refrigerator. Offerings from my benefactor. Bananas, grapes, tangerines. A note on the kitchen counter asks for receipts for everything I buy from now on—they need to track my expenses. I walk dizzily around the house…certainly a result of the procedures at the hospital. How long will the side effects last? Ah, the mirror, there is always the mirror to keep me honest: I have the face of a beast. The remains of my hair are disheveled, a heavy frown…an angry Beethoven without deafness or music. What I feel inside does not correspond to my disturbed face. I float on dizziness while my expression burns with sweat, blood pumping from my nostrils. Something tells me that I won't survive the wind outside, or London, or much less the trip back to Brazil. But they'll call me to the big conference and I'll tell them who they are. A knock on the door. It's the owner of the apartment, the Vietnamese man. His father owns half of Hackney. He wants to measure my bedroom window, the Englishman asked him to install curtains. The Englishman wants to hide me from the neighbors. They'll take away my view of that dry tree readying itself for spring. I ask him to come in. He is very young and doesn't like to talk. I sit on the bed and he takes the window's measurements. I'll have him once more when he installs the curtains. He doesn't look me in the eye. It occurs to me to grab the edge of the sheet and wipe my bleeding nose. I apologize to the Vietnamese man, the owner of the apartment. I tell him this has happened with my nose since I was a child. I say I'll make some tea. He says that he can't today. He'll take some when he comes back with the curtain. He shuts the door behind him. Will he really come back and cover the window? I pick up some fruit: grapes, mandarins, cherries, strawberries, and wrap them in the tablecloth… People start coming in, I peer through the curtain, onto the scene where I'll utter the words they expect from me… I don't know what to do with that bundle of fruit in my lap. I'm waiting backstage for the conference to start. I lie in bed with the fruit on top of me. I see blood on the pear from my nasal stream. I fall into a heavy sleep. The Vietnamese man is not gone yet. Or has he come back? He looks at me from the bedroom doorway and asks if he can come in to measure the window. I murmur yes. He wears a pair of jeans and a blue hooded jacket. I see him from behind, his close hair-cut shining black. The Vietnamese man turns to me and says the curtain will be ready in three days. I try to get up and walk him to the door, though this etiquette is not necessary since this is his house. I sneak out, hugging the walls; he descends the stairs at a fantastic speed. When I get to the door I see bright lights outside. The evening is shining crazily. I think everything is the result of the hospital procedures. I close the door. My shirt is stained with blood. Where's the bull I had been carrying with me?

I was a soldier, wounded by circumstance. But the war was not over, and I pressed forward. Even if climbing those steps back to bed ended up costing me my life. My vision was cloudy. At the top of the stairs, the Englishman looked at me. He could indeed show up at any moment—I had to live with that possibility… I knew I was not even a tenant in my own body any longer, a piece of me had stayed behind, lying in that hospital bed, and I was aware that I was no longer a tenant of my apartment either: here was the owner, suddenly knocking on the door to take the window's measurements, here was

the Englishman at the top of the stairs, before I had
the time to clean myself up in what I had until now
considered to be my home… My vision was cloudy,
but I already knew his silhouette by heart. I scram-
bled up the steps, not knowing what action the
Englishman would take when he got close. Would
he take me back to the hospital, put me to bed, or
throw it in my face that I was no longer part of his
plans?

Just before I reached the top of the stairs, I
fell. I clung to his shoes, dirt was stuck to them by
London's humidity. I clung to them as a wounded
soldier would cling to the trunk of a tree so he
might rise again and continue to rage in battle. This
Englishman had definitely changed my life, and I
would make that clear to him with every minute I
still had left. I would completely dedicate myself to
his plan. We were in the same battalion, and it didn't
matter how much the invading army pressed me to
negate everything I had tried to be. Name, nationality, race, religion. It was numbing trying to make
sense of the new elements of my citizenship. I was
that classic character with nothing left to lose. With

nearly nothing, I could be a king. For me, someone was sleeping in the Bloomsbury hospital. At this point, I didn't know if I would wake up. I could only count on myself, here, clutching the Englishman's dirty shoes. He pulled away. I drooled more and more, as if weeping from my mouth. My eyes still resisted clarity. They were my two sentinels, seeing only fog. I crawled into bed. I dragged myself up onto the blankets and laid on my belly with great difficulty. Lying on my stomach, I stayed. My eyes didn't want to close. They stared at the lilac wall as if wanting to retain that color for all eternity. I felt a warm weight descending over my body. It lulled me down, hot and comfortable, until I fell asleep…

I could say I fell asleep because I definitely lost consciousness. It was as if a factory of ideas, memories, and dreams collapsed upon me in bed. Surely I could not call that sleep. The weight of that clash of images pushed itself onto me, tossing my body and mind around at its whim, and I sensed that when I woke up I would be reincarnated as a result of this weight, whose appearance I couldn't discern without risk of interrupting the transformation.

Bewildered, I woke and sat up. The covers and sheets seemed to have barely survived a hurricane. Why had I accepted this suffering? Why didn't I rejoice in noticing that my hard cock had come back to life? My chest, my arms…of a modest gymnast. Would I know how to stay awake? I walked naked around the house to see if I would run into anyone. There was no sign of any presence. I opened the refrigerator. I drank water from a bottle. I leaned against the kitchen sink. Showing off my cock. It was the first time in so long that I had felt uncontrollably horny. Right there I relieved myself in three, four strokes. I fell on the floor with my sperm spilled on the tile. Another damned police car drove by with its loud siren… From now on, I would have all the sex I wanted in London. I would have fun, I would pass the time, while I waited for the Englishman and his invisible cabal to decide what to do with me. Why couldn't I be like any other Englishman? I would do anything for a British passport—I was sure that by now I would never find my Brazilian passport again, even if I searched all over the house. I had shoved it into some hole in my memory. I ran my finger through the thin semen and sang an old Carnival song. Wasn't today, after all, Fat Tuesday?

From the kitchen window, I watched my Turkish neighbor resting on his bed, watching TV in the early evening. My drunken companion at the pub had complained about his wife, but the Turk here seemed just to want to rest, surely feeling at home in this country for some time now. A feeling I didn't have. I didn't rest, didn't stroll around with my weapons set aside, and didn't work. Everything exerted itself indifferently, forcing me to prove myself. The Turk remained in his bed. I doubted he fully understood what the Brits were saying on the TV. I had seen him on the street with his countrymen speaking their language. Nothing else caught his attention beyond his memories of the fatherland and the images on the screen. I wanted to be him for a moment, there, devoted only to resting at home. I was beginning to realize that I had fled from a situation in Brazil. I was not sure which one—"where is my memory?" I had authored books; I had brought them here. I ran to the living room. There they were above the mantel. I didn't regret them. But, yes, they had stolen time from me so that they could be standing there. Of course, it was because of them I was in England. It was for them that I no longer wanted to go back to where they had sprouted. I couldn't be seen exactly as an amnesiac, but I was nothing but the discarded pulp of my books. Ah, I wish they could return wholly to my mind here in this distant country. And that they would add themselves up within me, so I could extract from them the eloquence I needed to earn my bread. I approached them, I ran my hand over each volume, but I realized I had become illiterate. Their titles didn't tell me anything, their letters were frigid. I touched the dusty covers: yeah, not so long ago I was living for them, because of them.

The phone rang. A man named Mark, a professor of Latin American Studies at Empire University, asking me for an interview. I looked at the editions lined up on the mantel and said, "Okay." He invited me to pay him a visit and have dinner afterward. When he gave me his address, a street that goes from London Bridge toward the south side of the city, I realized I was excited again. I'll make a pact with the mirror, I murmured, hanging up the phone. I won't look at my image anymore, and in return, I'll keep wanting more. I ran into the bathroom, picked up the mirror, and flipped it over. I would be faceless; I would avoid any reflection of my features. Blind to my own image, I would reinvent myself through those who had no investment in my face. That would become my task in London since I had a bus pass for another five days and could travel around the city. In any case, the mirror was still there, hanging backwards but there; and if I had to run away tomorrow or the next day, I could still take a last look at myself to remember whom I was carrying with me.

I left to visit the professor well before it was time. I went down to the city center. I crossed London Bridge on foot, the Thames rippling in the cold wind. I didn't know this part of the city so I walked around. I found an old market. Rabbits, lambs, fish hanging upside down. Cheese, vegetables. I went into a cathedral they said Shakespeare frequented. I walked down its center aisle. In the second row, an old man was blowing his nose. I heard someone call,

Sir, sir. I turned around, and it was the man, gesturing for me to take my cap off. I turned away from him with my hat still on my head, I was not going to take it off, no, no. The old man came running after me. I hurried on. Just as I felt I'd escaped from his chase, once again on the outskirts of the market, a few sudden drops began to fall, something common in the city at this time of year. I felt it necessary to be there, catching the drizzle that didn't really get me wet. I felt it necessary to kill time—in fact, I didn't care if I had been killing time during my entire stay in London, I had come to this edge of the world for that, to occupy an intermission without end. To some degree meeting Professor Mark would create a situation I could embrace with open arms, without thinking about how the winter afternoon was fading quickly and if I stayed away from the house on Mare Street for too long I would not be able to work the lock when I returned home. Ah, there was still an hour left before my meeting with Professor Mark. I tried to smile at the passersby, trying to give a general sense that I was well and happy. Many people responded. They smiled, too. Especially the elderly. Some even showed their yellow teeth, their delusions of teeth.

If everything went as I hoped, Professor Mark would become someone that supported me in the city. He would speak of his sleepless night, of his little health problems. And I of mine. If he was counting on me having something to say about my books, of course, he would be disappointed to the extent that he would then try to avoid me. But if we were to become friends, if he were to show me the ins and outs of London as if I were dear to him, I could wait more comfortably for the Englishman's decisions. I would have fun with Professor Mark; we would exchange our impressions about this stage of our lives, because I'd bet he was around my age, although he was a man with more direction in life. I'd bet he was already thinking about retiring, while I doubted I would ever reach a situation like the retirement that Professor Mark was preparing himself for. The main thing is—I told myself—I am innocent and should not be penalized. Why did I say this at this moment, waiting to cross a street where I needed to look left while in Brazil I was supposed to look right in the same place? Sometimes, absurd ideas came into my mind, and they were the ones that nurtured me the most, that gave me nourishment for three or four days. I am innocent, I repeat, innocent, and Professor Mark will shake my hand warmly and we will talk for the whole afternoon.

I rang the bell. A few seconds later, he opened the door. We smiled as if we had been waiting for this meeting for a long time. He seemed, yes, to be my age. My first impression: a vital man; not like me, given to melancholy. He brought me into the kitchen, he had just returned from the old market I had discovered while killing time before our visit. He wanted to organize the vegetables he had bought. Then he opened several tins of tea, asked me to smell them and choose the best to drink while we talked. Oh, I sighed, this one, it comes from those fields we never step on. He asked me if I wanted to go to India with him…there were cheap flights. I could leave it all behind if I wanted to: Palermo, why not? Sicily… With him, I would even want to go to hell, because, together, we could extract a sweet taste from everything—like the tea that was promising with its aroma. How have people like the two of us—ripe in extremis, almost to the point of falling off the branch—met here in paradise? We sat in the living room drinking tea. We could hardly control ourselves in our contentment. I unbuttoned my coat, took off my scarf, my hat. If he let me, I'd get naked. The temperature was perfect, not denying us the sensation of paradise. I saw my books lined up in a handy place. I cooled off. Mark said he had heard of my visit to London from an acquaintance, but right now he needed to take a shower. He asked me to come to the bathroom with him to continue our conversation. Mark was not merely a benevolent man. He was going to take a shower and I would watch his demonstration of cleanliness or whatever while sitting on the toilet, verifying that he was still in shape. As he began undressing I noticed—somewhat euphorically, as if I was, at last, allowing myself to see my new self in a mirror—I noticed the firmness of his ass, and his belly, not flaccid, only vaguely prominent. His sack, though a little enlarged as it is the case for men our age, seemed to shrink as I looked at it, as if it were giving a very private performance. I would bring the vegetables from the kitchen into the bathroom, to compose the scene of that endless undressing by a man my age. I would photograph him surrounded by vegetables before he got in the bathtub, as he bathed, and then as he dried himself off, surrounded by beets and carrots; bay leaves for his crown as the emperor of London; the afternoon was cloudy and icy outside. I was beginning to think that staying in London and watching this man undressing would keep me from my suffering. Suddenly, I thought that keeping my clothes on was a waste. It was necessary to pay homage to the situation. Mark was singing British songs from the '40s and '50s. At the end of each song he would name the artist and the date.

He stopped singing at last. He fixed his gaze on me and invited me to join him in the bathtub. Oh, I've never known how to share my nakedness with anyone. That's what I said. I shrank almost to the fetal position. And after so many years (that I remembered)…I cried. Yes, I couldn't help it. With my face tucked between my legs I felt my pants get wet with tears. There, sitting on Professor Mark's

toilet, whom I had just met and who showed me
his nakedness in the soapy bath, I couldn't help but
create a ridiculous scene with my crying. I stopped
before I entered the sobbing phase. Professor Mark
wore a towel over his shoulders like a cloak and
seemed perplexed by my behavior. I raised my head,
dried my eyes with my hands, and tried a yellow
smile. I felt like an eight-year-old boy in front of an
authority on genetics…I don't know. It didn't feel
like this man was a scholar of my work asking me
for an interview for his research. In front of him, I
felt like a useless man, a miserable scribbler of dead
hours. He offered me his hand to lift me from the
toilet. He felt I was receding into some distant point
and that it would be harder to catch me later. It was
necessary to revive myself here, now. Little did he
know that the tears I shed were a good sign. Of
what exactly, I had no idea. But something crystal-
line in me had softened and flowed, it was gone. All
ridiculous, I know, why repeat it? He pulled me by
the hand and kissed me. It was a prolonged kiss between his mouth and my cheek—and in those seconds I felt, slowly, the temperature of human flesh

again, after such a long time. The mucus on his lips nearly burned as his tongue licked the remains of the salty moisture from my face. We felt there would not be much more than that kiss—if we could call it a kiss—which those two ripened men had shared. Professor Mark, I thought... And he might have thought: Ah, this Latin American writer...

There could be no dinner with Professor Mark now. I'd make some excuse—I don't like being out at night, something like that. My tearful sentimentality had been too much for one day. Why do people visit each other? I wondered. If they stayed home embroidering like in the past, doing some handiwork, they would gain more. Professor Mark hugged me at the front door. I had met someone peculiarly different than the normal Englishman. Later, I learned he was brought up in Italy. Was that the difference which made him hug me like that? I hugged him too, willingly. Since I would have to become more than I'd ever been before, I let it happen. Professor Mark had gotten dressed; under our clothes, our genitals touched. An intimacy that was lost in time: it would not have occurred to me any other time; I had never cultivated such an idyll, given in to such simple seduction. My mind tingled and the sensation trickled down to the nape of my neck, everywhere. Would he be the person to defend me if I needed it? And would I need it? Then allow me to ask for help, here, now. Bye, Professor, I stammered, and he stammered, bye. And he opened the door onto the windy street for me.

Why was I a man running away? I asked myself, buttoning my coat, wrapping the scarf around my neck. I'll leave Hackney, I mused. I will come here, make a nest with Mark; I still have an old car in Brazil to sell, almost nothing, I know, but with that money I could spend about three months here subsuming myself in kisses and hugs with the professor. Then I'd repack my bags, I don't know, and die on my trip back to Brazil. Three months, three months, repeated like a litany I needed to hear to calm myself down. I sat in a family-owned Chinese restaurant. They worked incessantly, one could not imagine them during leisure hours. The restaurant was bubbling with customers. I had made a move to leave, but a staff member found me a lonely table in the far back, a single chair pressed between the wall and the tablecloth. And wouldn't this be the solution for our ills? Throw ourselves into daily work like good ants... Have a good sleep as a reward... They spoke loudly with each other, surely exchanging information related to the service. The matriarch, seated near me, wouldn't leave her royal post, giving orders, pointing out details that only a general would observe.

I had lost a great deal of time taking in the scene, but I felt refreshed. The testimony, if there were any, was not in action—it was inscribed on pages forgotten on the grass, open to the wind, restless, before swirling sand buried them in the churlish heart of the earth.

I went out into the night without wanting to take any sort of transportation. I would cross London Bridge, cover a portion of the city; if I crossed through to the north, northeast, I would hit Hackney. I thought of myself as a cowardly creature who, in the face of the enigma that was the Englishman who had brought me to London, could only be silent and wait. I was coming from a stupid bout of tears, sitting on Mark's toilet watching him bathe. Yes, tears had rolled down my face when he invited me into the tub with him. Stupid, huh? How could I go back home after that? I would walk all over London, all over the United Kingdom, if it would wipe away that cowardice of my tears. I crossed London Bridge, bent against the wind and drizzle. I came upon the first avenues of the city center, passing by centuries-old churches squeezed in between modern buildings. Sometimes I would sit on the steps of a church, rehearsing with a cupped hand begging for alms in the cold night, or lying on the stone floor, pretending to be dying from exposure, suffering from acute malnutrition, being the most abandoned of beggars. I had been built for that life—I knew it since I was a child—and not for receiving meager stipends from European institutions. That was my condition, to die, frozen on the streets of London, perhaps heaving a great sob in the end, losing consciousness in a way that would feel like an orgasm that traveled up to the dome of my brain before exiting through my mouth. Oh… through my mouth that smiled at my condition.

Sometimes, somebody or other passed by, certainly thinking I was just a drunkard, since I was wearing my normal clothes. But I kept my cupped hands extended, without saying a word, secretly asking for nothing, or just for a little, for something that those walking along the sidewalks were accustomed to denying. If I ran to Mark's house, threw myself into his arms, time would pass. But did I want to throw myself into Professor Mark's arms and stay nested in them like a drenched goldfinch? Keep begging for one more chance in London? Gullible, I had come to London because of a salesman of illusions who, for some reason I still needed to discover, had chosen me as the heir to the British chimera. I coughed; I was indeed getting sick under that insistent drizzle, but I didn't want to leave. If the police came to talk to me and took me to a shelter, I might bow my head gratefully. Like a citizen who had adopted Chinese ways of greeting from now on. Hands on my chest, my head bowed in reverence. I'd be a comrade to the English police. I'd become an informer on discreet drug dealers so they wouldn't deport me. No, no, I didn't want to leave London's dampness. Let the Englishman who had called me to Great Britain's atmosphere forget me, and Professor Mark, too. I was just going to stay here, fasting, on this step.

Professor Mark told me during his bath that, during a certain summer of his youth in Bellagio, on the shores of Lake Como, he had experienced his first adventure in love. A village girl, religious in a daily mass kind of way, with whom, one afternoon, he went to a stable he knew to be abandoned. He promised the girl they would make a nest and make an exemplary family; they would live in London, and she would get to know the great city; she would learn a new language, and he would provide her with a fireplace, satin lingerie, parties in royal circles. But once the girl was lying in the hay, anxiously awaiting his advances, he retreated, he told me, buttoning himself up and turning away to follow a grateful, busy, single life, one with bountiful love affairs, as he was then already a boy who had long ago stopped wearing breeches, while I still hadn't even thought of becoming the writer he wanted to get to know better. I would go on fasting, sitting on that step, detached from all the movement on the street, having unlearned how to react even if they touched me, beat me, gave me a hand…

I heard a groan… I looked around… On the steps of a portentous building, just ahead of me, a young man with dreadlocks seemed injured. Blood on his throat. I removed his scarf, and with it tried to remove the clots that hid the exact size of the wound: it was huge, maybe a shot…no, certainly a stab. Would I know how to treat him? I'd be his nurse; I'd heal him on the sidewalk in two or three months, only by the strength of our friendship. I think I went crazy that night… I won't argue, but the fact is that I was already hugging him; I was holding him to my chest and he began to whisper. I brought his mouth to my ear, staining myself with blood, and I heard: It was him… The guy was feverish on that cold night, and it gave me heat. My life was suddenly thrown in with his, into that embrace with the possibly dying young man. It didn't matter; my life could have been thrown in with anything that came my way on the streets of London. The young man finally expired in my arms. I realized it because his head fell back and

so remained, a desistance I only knew how to re-
hearse. I squeezed his hand. His mouth opened, and
I could see the pool of blood that had overflowed
his rotten teeth. That death, in some way, in some
corner of my mind, gave me tremendous satisfac-
tion. Someone was not afraid to go all the way to the
end. To do for others what everyone tried to avoid. I
wished I could follow him, but I didn't have his brav-
ery; I lacked the necessary elements to consummate
the act. I needed that hug today. No, no, I would not
go back to the apartment in Hackney; on the streets
of London I was going to resist until I too might
triumph. Listen…wasn't I the bull?

I supported the boy's head on my legs. I heard a
police car's siren. I moaned: Let the cops not come
near us. The pool of blood began to spill. The siren
faded away. I lay the dead man on the step. I hid the
bloodstain on my scarf, rewrapping it around my
neck, and kept walking. I crossed neighborhoods.
I smiled at some of the passersby so they wouldn't
suspect the drama I carried on my scarf. I didn't
want to throw it away yet, as if at some point in
the future I might still prove to myself that I hadn't

been such a coward, that I still carried some of the
warm essence of the dead man with me, that I had
not abandoned him entirely. I smiled; my smile was
sometimes a sickening grimace, to set me apart a
little more. I was passing through Bloomsbury.
Down Oxford Street. I got to Soho. There was a
black woman in white panties and bra at the door
of a whorehouse. She whispered something to me.
I stopped. She had a firm body, entirely beautiful.
She said she had a room upstairs…very, very warm,
with a fireplace. Yes, that was what I needed. She
sat on the bed, called me over to her, asked me for
the money in advance. When I grabbed the wallet from my pocket, my pen fell, and so did several
receipts I was keeping for the Englishman. I paid
her. She opened a drawer in the bedside table and
put the pound notes inside. In bed, I lay my head
on her legs. From between her legs came the heavy
scent of some extravagant perfume. That odor was
impregnating and took away my desire to do anything other than to lie there, getting more and more
drunk on the fragrance passing up my nostrils; perhaps I could fall asleep until my hour was up. She

ran her hand over my head and didn't try anything else. She kept caressing my hair and spoke in a certain African tongue. From Kenya, she said when we said goodbye. Those words without semantics worked as a mantra for me. And, as such, they were hypnotic, leading me to a state of indeterminacy: a silky whisper that never blossomed into gesture or action. Of course, I would have stayed in the arms of that black geisha for the rest of my life if she had let me. I would have given her three times the money if I'd had it so I could stay a whole day submerged in that sub-ecstasy. I would leave there healed, ready to accept anything, and to go all the way to the end without looking back.

But she squeezed my shoulder and shook it lightly. I understood. I got up slowly. I descended the stairs like a drunkard, running my hand over the wall, looking for support. The day had broken. I walked and walked…I was in Soho Square. I passed an open church. I went in and sat for a while. There was a small line for Communion. I hadn't been hungry at all; I was one step away from anorexia. But putting a warm Communion wafer in my mouth

that early in the morning seemed like a good idea.
I got in line. When my turn came, I stuck out my
tongue and immediately the thin white wafer, almost nothing, began to dissolve in my mouth. So
quickly, I thought, with hardly any taste. I sat down,
leaning back in the front pew, and fell asleep.

Sir, sir, said a devout Catholic lady, bent over
me. It might have been early afternoon. *Hmmm,* I
said, *hmmm,* and I waved my arm in a gesture as
if shooing curious people away. The woman backed
off with large steps. I hadn't forgotten that I needed
to get rid of my scarf, stained with the Rastafarian
man's blood. I was not exactly illegal in this country,
but it wasn't advisable for a foreigner in a state of
confusion like I was to have somebody else's DNA
on his belongings. This is the fate of cowards: to get
rid of the evidence of any experience that does not
bring along with itself a greater justification. They
don't participate in anything; they simply hint at
some higher human aptitude, in fear of any misunderstanding.

So I let the scarf slip, fall to the floor, between
one pew and another. If the devout woman found it,

she would think it belonged to me—yes, a wounded man who had fallen asleep in the church and who, disturbed by feverish nightmares, shooed her away. And wasn't I living in a feverish nightmare after all? What would be my next step? I started walking again, passing through Covent Garden; a group of young people played Mozart; I stopped and gave them a coin then suddenly decided to give them two; I looked up as the sun came out after being hidden for weeks; I wanted to scream for joy, to faint, to be taken once again by chance to the hospital in Bloomsbury... Was someone really staying there in my bed? And was he just waiting for me to come back and give him my place out here? The day had come. Either I gave up on myself so that I could be the other, or...I don't know, I'd have to spit in the face of the first passerby and let his anger get beyond consideration of consequences. Understand? I asked the air. No, no one could understand, let alone I, who was escaping from the situation that had brought me to London and to which I no longer knew what service I had to give. And had I ever known, huh? People on the street looked at me as if they saw a ghost. Huh? Huh? I was opening my arms as if dancing an irrefutable ballet, passing a hand over my genitalia occasionally, as if to accentuate the spring heat, the blooming.

Some people stopped and smiled, others made faces of pity. I heard timid claps. I abandoned my lonely ballet and headed toward the place I thought I had to overcome. If I passed that point, I wouldn't have to deal with anyone anymore. What point? I didn't even know, I only knew that I no longer wanted to have anything to do with that truncated invitation to stay in London. Nevertheless, I didn't want to leave the city. Never! I lacked the memory of my bed in Brazil…, there's always Hackney, right? I asked a passerby who turned out to speak Spanish and who commented that, yes, he could understand me quite well. He had the same mental register as me. He knew what was going on long before he saw me. He was pedaling a rickshaw for the tourists wandering around the neighborhood. He was Chilean. He told me to climb on, he would take me to wherever I wanted to go. On the seat was a thick, fuzzy blanket. I wrapped myself up in it, and he pedaled me away. This is good, I said after many laps. I gave him my coins. It was drizzling. How handsome this Chilean was. Such features! I felt a desire to kiss that face. If the kiss popped close to his ear, even better. His ear came from the gods. Instead, I kissed his hand. If the house in Hackney was still at my disposal, would he want to go there and share the bed? No? There was so much I wanted to ask. But a French couple asked him for a ride. And there they went, making me swallow my thousand questions…

Wasn't it time for me to take the 55 to Hackney and see if the house was still mine? If the Englishman who had brought me to London had left another of his notes? Hopefully not a final one…canceling my permission to be in the city. Hopefully I was not homeless all of a sudden. Because I would never use the return ticket to Brazil. At the same time, I couldn't see how my official or semi-official stay in this country could continue. I could only hope then that this impasse lasted for the rest of my days here. That I could keep a roof over me, paid for by them, and continue receiving the minimal funds from them that guaranteed me food and transportation around the city so I could warm myself up at the National Gallery—enjoying Van Gogh, seated on a bench some afternoon, or appreciating Cézanne some other day, circling to keep myself a little warmer. That, of course, would have been my ideal life, and the English people might provide it to me because of some permanent misunderstanding, born of some state and/or cultural secret impossible to extricate. Why did I avoid taking the 55 and facing my destiny? Would I spend another night on the street? Wasn't I old enough for this extravagance? More extravagant than if I had to live illegally in London, working hard at God knows what—me, accustomed to writing books. The right thing to do was to write a letter requesting an undetermined, provisional period to myself. And at the end, I would discover a way to die, that's it!

But I couldn't see myself walking toward the 55 stop on Oxford Street. I was on my way to the palace where the Englishman had taken me directly from the airport as soon as I arrived in London. It was on Jermyn Street. Its construction began in the seventeenth century and ended in the eighteenth. The building had no inscriptions. A flag of the United Kingdom fluttered. The building's haughtiness didn't resemble that of a university. It looked more like a diplomatic building. Who had invited me? Once again I opened the letter I always carried in my pocket in case the police stopped me. There was the signature of the Englishman who had invited me. Underneath his signature were the initials of the institution he represented, handwritten, with no stamp. At the time of the invitation, I thought about asking somebody in Porto Alegre about it, or calling someone in Rio, Sao Paulo, something. But I didn't know anyone. I called the British honorary consul in Porto Alegre. I faxed him the letter so he could tell me if I would pass through immigration without any problems with it in my hands. He only recommended that the invitation letter should not mention money. He asked me if I smoked or liked to eat well, because if I was like that, what they were paying me wouldn't make it past the third of the month. I did not pass along the consul's concerns to the Englishman, who had already sent me the plane tickets. Yes, the order for me to pick up the tickets had already been issued, then I had the tickets in hand; I had no doubt this Englishman and the group he represented wanted me to come to England because of the books I had written—they had shown that they had, at least, the means and a clear desire to support that story.

I looked at the imposing building where the Englishman who had invited me should be. The wear and tear that my body might have suffered over the course of the dragging, endless days of my stay seemed irreversible. My reputation might have fallen so low that the only way out was for them to escort me back to Brazil. But why? I wondered. What had corroded things to this point that it was too late to turn back? Or was it not like that at all? Were they doing what was best for me? I scratched my genitals like an idle man in the full orgasm of a Taurus fantasy. I should go back to Hackney now, stay in my room, recover from last night's lack of sleep with a beautiful rest, and when I awoke, I would receive glorious news that would justify my entire stay in London. But would I like that to happen? To fully understanding would imply imminent departure. No, no, I should keep simmering slowly, and hope that the decisive moment of my return to Brazil would only come when I succumbed once and for all to the afflictions I had lived until then.

It was then that I saw myself running through Piccadilly Circus, scaring doves, forcing people to make way. I crossed Soho in a rush, ran a length of Oxford Street, along came the 55 to carry me to the truth. I got on, went to the upper deck. Inside, they were speaking Portuguese, Persian, Chinese, Vietnamese, English, Spanish, Italian, Turkish. What had they all come to do on these streets, which, as Hackney approached, grew increasingly ugly, dirty, and beset by endless construction? I had serious doubts they lived better in these London ghettos than in their meager birthplaces. What set me apart from them was that I was trying to indefinitely prolong a stay that, providing me almost nothing, didn't ask for anything in return. It asked only for the cost of my vigil. But when would an opportunity like this happen for me again? I would

make a pact, I'd said already, that when the arrangement became unsustainable for the institution, I
would commit hara-kiri in their offices if necessary
so no one would doubt that my debt was fulfilled. Or
else I would stop eating, spend all the money from
the miserable grant on amphetamines, never closing my eyes again to further diminish my lifespan,
and consequently my expense to them. I would live
my last days as a vagabond, wandering the streets
of London, through the museums with free admission, with my amphetamine-bloated brain hover-
ing above the daily lives of the mortals. Having my
house in Hackney, the little money at the end of the
month… I descended to the bottom level of the bus
as my stop neared, feeling my lips dry up, my hand
tremble. It was now or never. And this inexorable
situation would kill me before my time, ending the
joy of this untranslatable stay abroad.

I walked toward the house in Hackney like
someone who was going to save a shipwreck survivor, slowly performing the necessary measures to
avoid shocking his system. One situation was that
the Englishman who had called me to London

might be waiting in the house, another was that my key night not open the changed lock, and a third hypothesis was that a powerful committee would be waiting for me there, to not only disavow me but also take away my temporary freedom. Fool, I told myself repeatedly, how foolish you are for believing in blessings.

The key still fit in the lock. I childishly thought I would find peace there again. As soon as I closed the door behind me, I heard the clatter of cutlery. There was someone in the kitchen. I galloped upstairs. The Englishman who had invited me to London was sitting at the table with a woman, having a meal. He introduced me to her, an employee. He filled a glass of wine and offered it to me. I accepted, but I didn't drink it. I realized that things were beginning to take a different tack in regard to the members of that organization. A real dysfunction: the figurehead of a British entity invites me—the author of seven books—for a stay in London, providing a house and some money; but then I arrive at that house and he's having a meal with some woman with whom his relationship is unclear, at least as far as the institution is concerned. It's another chapter, I thought. Can I use this situation to my benefit? I could cover up their clandestine relationship that was going against their entity's rules, which felt like those of a paramilitary organization. Let them use my kitchen, my bedroom; I'll sleep in the living room, or in the kitchen even; they'll have the bathroom…all the rooms with heating. As long as the relationship lasts, my residency will be guaranteed. Meanwhile, my shame will flow from me as I sleep to disappear down the drain. When they wake up, there'll be no trace of me. And I wouldn't have to go back to Brazil. It would all be so beneficial to me. And for them, too? They invited me to sit down. She was beautiful and blonde. She served me a chicken breast, two, three vegetables I hadn't experienced in Brazil. I remained silent throughout the meal. Any urge to speak that came up in my throat dissolved at the slightest tentative movement of my tongue. My words would disturb. I needed to become invisible sooner than later, I thought. For now, I was going to lie down in the corner of the living room and pretend to sleep. I'd leave my room to them so they could have their orgy…that's what I'd do. If I had to dream to prove I was asleep, who knows, I would end up dreaming if my body reached the limit of resistance. Perhaps, everything could be possible in the dream, unlike here, and thus I'd be able to rest, and get new and different results. My tiredness did not demand sleep, but, damn!, how I craved some indistinguishability between bodies, volumes, and formats. Was this the night my wish would be granted? I would fall asleep with some other identity, and they would not find me: I would be disguised not only among them but distributed throughout the entire house in Hackney. I would be in the curtains, at the table, everywhere and nowhere at the same time.

I asked if they needed the room. They both looked at each other and smiled. Their libidos were running wild, and they didn't mind making me an accomplice. Okay…I had nothing against it. I excused myself. I turned off the lights in the living room. I did not take off my clothes. I lay in a corner, on the hard floor. The neon light of the Vietnamese restaurant bathed me in red. What I found at that moment was my exact measure, with it I could rest not only that night but in the future. Let the English couple enter the room at dawn, full of lust. Even now I was beginning to hear their giggles, their moans in the bedroom. I got comfortable; I curled up beside the radiator. I had no idea what I wanted anymore. Less, maybe? No matter what, I needed to accomplish it sooner rather than later, now…in London. I could no longer imagine my genitals burning and sending their missiles into the hell of someone else's entrails. And yet, curled up, my genitals were on fire. But just like the sunflower is ruled by the cycle of sun and stars, sleep would placate me. And it descended.

Early the next morning they had already left the house. In the bedroom, the blankets were in order, smoother than I generally left them over the sheets. In the kitchen, the dishes and pots were washed. I went to the living room window. At the corner of an alleyway, the two of them climbed aboard a truck that looked like it belonged to the British army. Many people were already settled in there, but I couldn't make out who they were. There was a tarp covering the back of the vehicle. The two of them climbed into the truck, their uniforms the dark and light greens and browns of camouflage, as if they were heading to some military exercise or even the war itself. They both carried a bag with their civilian clothes. But they weren't reacting as if they were doing anything all that serious, they were even smiling. It was the first time that the idea of going back to Brazil seemed appealing to me. That same day. Why was an English military officer interested in having me in England? What kind of service could I render to the diplomatic or military relationship between the two countries? This should not be the reason for me to give up now, I thought. If I had to collaborate, I would, as long as they told me why. What could not happen was to be forced to return to Brazil without my mission accomplished. To return, after being provided with housing and food for so long, without having given them anything in return…I could not allow that. I wanted to have a function: holy, diabolical, petty, innocuous, or heroic. And let that function have a geographically extreme distance, which I had to have crossed to end up here. Someone had committed the historic dirty trick of endowing a man with memories of Brazil, but I know those memories were about to expire. There were only two or three things left in my memory. Two or three things that made me shake my head. They clouded me; they clouded me to the point that I had to lie down, blanketed by fear. I was already dreaming, without knowing it. I was touching the skin of a mango in a tree. Even within the dream I knew it was a mirage, I had never been in that place. That I would shake my head and it would wake me up. I sat on the bed. I thought about the British Army truck. I went to the window. They were already gone. When the Englishman who called me to London returned, I would demand that he tell me everything. If the blonde came back with him, I would demand the truth from both of them. I would confess that my judgment had always been distractible, airy, that I lived in a world of floating things, but that I was no longer the same man. If they betrayed me, I would go to the English press and expose them.

I would provoke an international scandal.

They'd have to choose: either get rid of me or go fuck themselves—they and their whole gang. I fell to my knees, hugging the radiator. The heat was unbearable directly against my skin because I liked the rooms extremely warm. I moved away. How to move forward, hmm? I raised my arm, tried to touch something… No, it was nothing, just an illusion… The truth is that it was already dark and, bathed in red by the lights of the Vietnamese restaurant's sign, the room showed me signs of my confusion. I was an idle prisoner inside this cell. There was no point in turning on the light. I was a prisoner; I had nowhere to go. I could take the 55 again…go to Oxford Circus. But eventually I would have to return, and I had no other place to return to but here. I was at the mercy of the Englishman who had brought me to London. A prisoner, I lived in solitary confinement, sometimes dining with my jailer and his mistress. A privilege? I squeezed my eyes shut, blinding myself in the night's depths; I swore I was going to continue, to stay… There was a rigid nucleus inside me, something telling me: Yes! And my whole body hardened, standing on my feet, like it was made of bronze.

Then, from a simple bang, turmoil erupted. At first, because of the Vietnamese light, I saw everything as if covered in blood. I thought the war had fully come to London. Maybe I had been buried. Maybe everything had already occurred, and I was a survivor in his final hours. Days ago, trying to get out of the cold during one of my walks, I had seen a painting in the National Gallery, a picture by Bruegel of a suffering woman lying in bed, a crucifix resting on a pillow at her feet. And me, where would I look if in this same situation? Was there not some totem I could turn to in these final moments? I tried to imagine one, rushing, but nothing appeared to me, nothing, until it came up from the depths, slowly...a boat, and I was placed on it, and they took me through calm, gentle waters...

The fact is I was in a train station and not at the edge of a river. It was in a place called Hither Green. It seemed...yes...still a suburb of London. But I couldn't leave. It looked like it was a Sunday or holiday. It was almost deserted and the afternoon was abruptly fading. It was necessary to go up and down stairs to reach the platform that would take me back

to the city center. A young woman was trying to
maneuver a stroller. I asked if she needed a hand, already grabbing the other side of it. She seemed shy,
not saying yes or no. A child's voice under the can-
opy said thank you, effortlessly. I answered formally,
without being able to see the child. I completed the
task, and then looked for the train that would take
me to London Bridge station. It was taking forever;
there were far fewer trains scheduled that day. The
nearly empty station, getting more and more shad-
owy by the hour, was one of the saddest things I had
ever seen. From London Bridge station I would take
a bus to Hackney, without knowing what I would
find at home. I had thought of running away. But I
had gotten off at Hither Green, twenty minutes ago.
And now I was waiting for another train to take me
back to my prison. It was already evening when the
train arrived. Inside, I sat down. There was a young
man who stared out the window the whole time. For
him, the train's interior didn't seem to exist. His eyes
ran along the endless brick houses of the London
suburbs, little gardens in front; his eyes passed over
squares and parks, their bare trees, as if stunned by

the night; his eyes passed over what the window showed him to be real, as if he himself were generating the images—he had an expression of complete control over his creation: a small solitary god, whom I watched with something like devotion. This trip could last a lifetime because I would always have a new detail about him to observe: the small ring in the ear, the piercing of the lower lip, the absent-mindedness without posturing, the hood half-fallen, letting slightly wavy light hair appear. His foot on the seat in front of him. Until he noticed me. And I lowered my eyes, knowing that the train was approaching the London Bridge station. He got up, too. We stood side by side waiting for the doors to open. We headed in the same direction. We stopped in front of the same poster showing the schedules of several bus lines. If the two of us fix our attention on the same line, the night might show some promise...I thought to myself, impudently. In fact, not a single day passes that I don't imagine stripping the clothing from someone's body. That I never follow through with my desire, all the better...! Only picturing my hands opening buttons, the zipper, removing clothing piece by piece, unhurried… Then I realized the boy was no longer there. And I was relieved.

I got off in Hackney in peace. They might be occupied with their war activities. The house that night was mine. I passed by the alley where they had climbed into the army truck. Yes, I decided to go down the alley. Toward the chain-link fence in the back. Steel sheds. A plate engraved with something like ROYAL REGIMENT. Behind me, someone approached. He was a black man in an overcoat and woolen cap. He asked me if I knew what the army had been doing there. It used to be just an open field. The train passes in the background. Just then, I heard the sound of the train passing not far away. It had been sudden when the army came and set up the encampment. There are days when they disappear. No one knows why. This man who wanted to talk made me lose sight of the fact that I was in London. And the darkness gave me the sensation of having a chat on the side of some road… He still hadn't stopped talking about the reasons that would have made a whole regiment settle in that half-abandoned corner of Hackney. I saw myself as a country bumpkin who did not like to talk. Nothing frightened us there. Soon we'd be able to see shooting stars and more. And no one would say that we were standing in a neighborhood of immigrants in London, who had their hands on the chain-link fence guarding the place where a British army regiment spent time, every fifteen days or so they came, the man said. If that man were an undercover spy for the regiment, he wouldn't be getting a word out of me. Even if he was not... I chose not to talk. I had started talking late, when I was six. Suddenly, words had begun to come, in the backyard, talking to a tree. Here in London, on the edge of the regiment's quarters, listening to this man speak of some bellicose hypothesis that held little interest to me, I came to the distinct conclusion that life didn't want me to have optimal conditions, that's it. Life had given me seven books, that's true. But despite them, where was my autonomy? How long would I be the slave of this secret project without a glimpse of liberation? As I said, being a slave is not insurmountable, but one really does need to know to whom or what. The man was saying that the regiment was an anti-terrorist unit. That there were lethal antivenoms in there. I shook the chains of the fence lightly, as if my body burned and I was rolling in the grass to find relief. Ahhh! was the first thing I said. *What?* the man asked. I repeated, ah, ah, ah…! And another train passed. That *ah!* was not a moan brought on by tediousness. It sought to dramatize the man's words: Yes, the imminent danger that the two of us—no matter how much we talked and groaned—did not seem to be able to express, since we stood there like two men smoking cigarettes near warehouses of European extermination weapons. We were two poor peasants from the suburbs of the decision-making center. Should we keep hanging on the fence that separated that unknown military power from us mortals? And all this, just two blocks from my house. It was time for me to beget a child so she could tell me later whether or not I was right. I burst into laughter. And the black man burst into laughter. And the two of us walked away from the military post. When we reached the corner of the alley, each of us turned in the opposite direction. And the world did not end, and I went into my house—empty, empty, me alone with Bach to listen to on the radio I had brought from Brazil.

I lifted the blanket, sat, then laid my upper body down. The bed smelled of the sweaty flesh from those two the night before. It wasn't bad spending my sleeplessness breathing the fumes of bodies on fire. From time to time the kid constantly looking at the landscape on the train was beneath me and I bit him all over his body, even if he complained. From time to time Bach was a counterpoint from the heavens to the hell of my senses, playing heavily against my chaste destitution. My cum gushed out, toward the bedside lamp. Its shadow fell on my bedroom, and I went back to the aromas of the bed, which wouldn't let me fall asleep for the night.

And why fall asleep? To rest for what? If that black man had been inclined to not go into his cocoon but to stay, endlessly chattering to me about military power quarreling with the forces of terror, things like that, I would have liked to stay out all night under a sky that from time to time let one star or another slip away…as he had spoken it hadn't been the subject that enraptured me, but his baritone timbre, so rare to hear. It was not every night that you could have in your ear a voice that didn't need to sing even one entire song for you to understand it. As I breathed in the scent of the recent sexual activity from the sheets…as long as I was healthy, I would never tire of impregnating myself, as if I could feel myself birthing other selves, something like that. As I rolled on the sheets, I remembered the man as someone I would want to hear singing when the time for my final agony came. While Bruegel's dying virgin preferred to look at the crucifix as she died, I no longer wanted to see anything when my time came. I just wanted to listen to the unadorned melody of that man's voice. Suddenly, I was on all fours on the bed, like Rome's ancestral wolf feeding its babies, born from me in my solitary ecstasy. They were inebriated with my milk, yes, and excitement permeated my stay in London as if I wanted to impregnate it more and more.

The thermostat in the house was set to thirty degrees Celsius; I was sweating heavily. I jumped into an ice cold shower. I couldn't distinguish the heat of my body from the icy water. The thermal war was so colossal that I fell into the tub as if I had been electrocuted. I felt I needed someone to help me get up. But I was a solitary man, so I crawled out of the tub myself. I went to the bedroom. I fainted on the rug.

I heard a police car's siren. Another. I felt between my lips a substance with a jelly-like consistency. I opened my eyes with effort. With even more effort, I touched the thing in my mouth. Remains of vomit. It looked like a slab of bone marrow—it had been a while since I'd put anything in my mouth. It seemed I was feeling better—I might even have said sanctified—as if recompense were about to be given…for what I was not really sure, but it was as if the natural order of things—in which I had never believed—whispered that it was time to turn over the record. Understand? Something like that… Of course, it could all be a sign that I was going insane… this idea that I was entering some kind of oasis at last, after having tortured myself with the interior babble I'd been living with in London. I think I had suffered some type of ugly collapse in the tub. And when you come back from something like that, the little or almost nothing life usually gives you starts wanting to be extrapolated on, understand? You see yourself from higher up, in direct contact with luck; the beneficiary of a martyrdom that is nearing its end, or perhaps already over. I laughed. Even without the strength to laugh, I laughed at all this buffoonery my body was naturally enacting in its attempt to recover me. The Englishman who had brought me to London would continue his silence—in uniform or not—and the little bit of money I was being paid out of what seemed to be the British Government's coffers would no longer come, and suddenly I would be *homeless* in England unless they escorted me onto a flight back to Brazil. Was running away into the English countryside my only prospect? I asked myself, screamed it in my head, because my tongue was as hard as a cock, unable to emit a word. I'm going to a small town near Manchester, I'm going to work picking up debris in a junkyard, selling it to anyone who might be interested: my hands will be covered in blackened grooves; pubs will ban me for my bad smell; I'll sleep in my pigsty without removing the only clothes I own; I'll pay that price for wanting to stay here, until one morning I won't awaken, ending up in a common grave by Anglican mercy. I tossed and turned on the rug, naked, my mouth nasty from vomit. I couldn't get up. A horniness tried to wake me, I felt it, fluid that flowed down my spine, and when it reached its destination, it would make itself an accomplice to my cock, suffocate it since I was lying on my stomach in that moment. I managed to turn over, and my cock was the only part of my body that was revived. Where did it come from, this obstinate fire that didn't want to vanish? From London, my comrade, it was London that provoked this empire of the senses, and whose deep mystery seemed to bring me this pleasure that insisted on rising despite such an extreme situation of weakness and starvation. Done. I came, and at that moment a fine needle penetrated my brain, piercing, I know, another point that could now withdraw, certainly opening space for a greater night ahead. I was a reptile that still had the power to love. If another body were lying on the rug in my room in Hackney, like the boy who stared out the window on the moving train for example, I would fuck him and still want more. But if he asked me to bend over and kiss his navel instead, who knows, I would be unable to perform, even with groaning effort, the act of sitting up and bending my spine to extract from his navel the stench of that flesh he was denying me. I still loved, but I was a reptile, gentlemen: a being without the dorsal structure to live among its equals, except to fuck—lying down. And maybe I'd be this way forever. But what future could there be for a man resigned to the sole functions of fucking and ejaculating? Who would be inclined to continue this bland existence? All I could do was ask for help. However, I had no voice anymore. Now that… I wondered if I might be able to survive if I came again. So I began to think about the boy who looked out from the moving train, wishing he were here with me, wholly, I didn't care—all I could do was crawl. I was thinking about all these things, seeing if I could put an end to this joke: a good orgasm that would finish me once and for all—and then I'd be found, decomposing, when the British army finally decided to release that Englishman who was responsible for my last days in London. I focused my gaze out the window. It was snowing. It wasn't accumulating on the ground too much. But timid and scarce flakes were falling, yes. One day, I won't have anyone to tell today's episode to, but will I ever make it to that day? And why should those agonizing hours in London be kept for posterity? It was snowing, that was all. Looking at the snow, the extent of that fact did not negate my time. So what?—I was disgusted by my stupid mind games.

That's when I felt two hands catch hold of me like a shovel. And they brought me very close to a chest wearing a camouflage uniform. He examined me for a few seconds. He seemed not to mind me knowing about his relationship with the British Armed Forces. Then he put me to bed. And he made a call from the cellphone next to me. My hearing was not in perfect condition, like my vision and genitalia. As he finished the call, he reached down and took my wrist. He took my wrist with a puzzled frown, and I felt that I was going to escape from my conundrum, that they wouldn't want to see me fall into such a situation while I was in their hands. However, he just covered me. Turned off the light. I wouldn't mind having a prolonged recovery, as long as they were able to heal me. After all, if there was no cure, what was a mild discomfort like the one I was feeling…if I could just stay here, eating at least the bare minimum so that the days wouldn't end? Yes, and I wouldn't have to go back to Brazil, but stay here watching for the dry tree to bloom in the approaching spring… What good would it be for me to return to South America in full health if I didn't bring the smallest memory with me? The powers here in the UK felt I was their responsibility: They had created a role for me, and their attempt to heal me was the only way my success in that role was possible. I would know how to do it well, whatever its dimensions. They just needed to bring me back to perfect health, and I would be able to perform the thing they expected of me. But this time things would be different, because I was no longer the same; in explanation: if I did everything right, if I betrayed and fought and renounced and performed the crucial act, if I were, in short, the promised man, I would demand they let me stay here forever. I would claim my British nationality, retirement benefits…and other things that only my complete sanity would allow me to imagine. I turned around, managing to grab the second pillow and hug it. And I realized that I could already love this Englishman who was keeping watch over me from the next room as if he owned me… I don't know, I felt I could already love him like a friend to whom I owed my life. Now, yes, I felt ready to defend him to the end. All he had to do was come and give me orders. In that bed, I was being born again. Let them not ask me about the past, other nations, nothing else—I was just an assistant to the Englishman who was waiting in the living room for my cure to take place.

I spent days in bed. The secret gang who seemed to be keeping me in London gave no signal. One day I woke up with something being injected into my veins. It could only have been an IV because I didn't put solids in my mouth yet did not die. In the afternoons, a girl of about eight years old would come and offer me nuts, grapes. Eventually, I accepted. I don't know who she was. She would come in and out, jumping around the room. From time to time the Englishman who brought me to England showed up. He'd lift my blanket. He'd look either unfazed or disgusted. If disgusted, he'd take off the giant diaper I was wearing, continuing to look disgusted, and throw it in the trash. Then he'd come back with a damp cloth and clean me. These acts of cleansing lasted much longer than one might have expected from only his sense of duty. His features would normalize. He didn't leave any bruise on me unattended; he examined them, touched them, to the point where I'd get to look at my tree and wonder when it would start blooming again. Nature was starting to take on a new meaning for me. Enough of London, what I needed now was to go to the remote English countryside, be a fugitive among the cattle or a beast in a grotto, until I was shot by one of the locals who were frightened by my nakedness and colossal filth. The Englishman was still cleaning me, now obsessing over a little wound that wouldn't heal between my sack and anus; there, he ran his fingers over it, using the foam from some bathroom cleaning product, as if I were really made of the hard crust of an animal; such an animal like I truly aspired to be as he rubbed my wrinkled glans, my stinging asshole. My gaze kept returning to the bare tree, to the sky that never cleared, and I let this man in his warlike costume shuffle among my body parts as if he wanted to take the life from them, and not just semen.

Only once did I hear the voice of the child who sometimes fed me. It was certainly her, yes, calling someone named Bob. Was Bob the Englishman whom I only knew from his initials and whose last name was now lost from my brain? She called twice, three times, but no one answered. Was he a father who didn't like his offspring to call for him— therefore ignoring his daughter's voice? That day, I know the girl didn't show up in my room, leaving me slightly hungry for the little food I was gradually getting used to having. Then I realized it was night, and he came in with some of those pills that put me fast asleep. After he'd given me a glass of water to swallow the miscellany of medications, I remember feeling a joy…more…a euphoria, even while realizing that I was going to interrupt the thread of life that I mildly sustained in my hours of clarity.

I no longer felt trapped by a fear of waking up in Brazil. I felt that this place was mine, these sheets that he cleaned badly and sporadically with a cloth dampened with kitchen cleaner, all this was mine. It wouldn't be long before more of this country also belonged to me. I could be seen as a refugee without a cause. They'd end up seeing my case as urgent: I would only know how to survive if I stayed. He'd come with the medication in one hand; in the other, the glass of water. I was saved again. For him, I would do anything. Except get on a plane and leave.

There are so many planes in the London sky, I said, looking through the window. Counting them makes me tired on these sleepless nights. Dozens framed by my window. Oh, and what happened to the Vietnamese man who took the window measurements and never brought the curtains for the room? I was speaking again after being silent for such a long time, and I know he was quietly surprised. He was rejoicing without showing it. I could feel it when I looked directly into his eyes. If someone from the armed forces could read his eyes, they would fire him from his position immediately. His clear eyes were all he had at the moment with which to speak his mind: *Everyone expects you to come back, you little shit, and you'll come back, yes!* It was then that I leaned on his shoulders and said the name I thought was his: Bob… He answered that his name was not Bob. I let go of him and fell back onto the pillow which he had sprayed with some cologne to disguise the thousands of missed washings. When he switched off the light, I saw a plane pass the window again, this one going south. Before sleep knocked me out I played with my cock. It was a part independent of my body: always willing. True, it had been well washed—it didn't smell bad, nothing about it was diseased. It had been so long since I'd known what it was to have sex with someone. Or no? I got up without much difficulty. I supported myself on various things on my way to the living room. Bob— or whatever his name was—was standing there, fiddling with his pipe. What is it? he asked. And then he looked at my hard dick. That was something two men don't do: look at each other's dicks as one looks at a vase of flowers in a desert. He looked like that. On his face was a performance of mild surprise at seeing a man as weak as me being able to maintain a full erection. He told me to go to sleep; otherwise, the drugs would knock me down in the middle of the room. Yes, I gladly accepted. I was going to stay in London, damn the rest. As I went into my room, I looked back. He was staring at my ass.

The next morning he came to wake me up. He said we were going to visit someone who'd be good for my overall recovery. He took me by the shoulders and lifted me from the bed little by little until I stood. You're already better, he said. And this person will be able to improve your situation here. He opened the closet and took out my pile of clothes, which I hadn't worn the whole time I'd been bed-ridden, as I'd been either in diapers or naked. The clothes smelled bad, but even if I had any others, I wouldn't exchange them for anything: that shirt, those pants, the thick coat, all this had come so far with me in England; they were part of my way of being in this country, I wouldn't give them up for anything. He watched me dress as if it were part of his job to take note of what I wore or check to see that I was not carrying anything dangerous or

compromising with me, who knows. He continued to watch me dress like he could see in me the
true meaning of his days, that if he were alienated
from my existence he'd become worse than unem-
ployed—he'd be unable to even have the compan-
ionship of a woman, to bring her here to show her
his prey, yes, this one, this Brazilian who can't guess
his next move. Barton Street, he told the taxi driver.
I was sitting next to him in the car, trying not to fall
asleep. The pomp of London passing by—Trafalgar
Square, Parliament, Westminster—made me dizzy,
made me feel inadequate to the cause they might
still be inclined to include me in. The car stopped
on a street where the silence was golden. No, no one
came to look through the window to see whose car
was daring to disturb their distinguished ghosts.
Yes, the bells of Westminster tolled, not far away.
Before we entered the house the cab had stopped
in front of, the man gestured for me to look at who
had lived a few houses ahead: There, in a building
just like the one in which we would be welcomed.
I saw the plaque: HERE LIVED T. E. LAWRENCE –
LAWRENCE OF ARABIA – 1888–1935. Without

anything to do, I straightened my collar. One leg shivered, almost buckled. He rang the bell. An albino woman answered the door. She had the look of a servant. *Mister...* He didn't complete the phrase before she cut him off: He's waiting for you in the office, come in. He was a big man in a coal black wool suit. He didn't get up from his desk to greet us. He stretched his arms. Only then did he approach us. Me, in particular. He looked at me with such intensity it was as if he could see me inside. But there was no real transparency in his expression. Only a concentration in his gaze, which one usually doesn't have unless one is faced with the presence of someone of dubious quality. The man being observed was me. But as long as that condition served to keep me in London, then fine, let him continue to look. But what exactly was the meaning of this gentleman's gaze? He seemed all-powerful to me. What was it he was examining so intently? I have always been an ordinary man, have only written seven books, that's all... The two of them looked at each other. From their exchanged gazes I couldn't deduce anything. It was a beautiful afternoon outside, the winter sending signs of giving in, but behind the man in the fireplace a fire still smoldered, almost dead. In the giant frame beside him, an image of hunting: several gentlemen mounted, a dog with a rabbit between its teeth. In the figure of the old man—who continued to examine me—there was imprinted a portrait of pain, perhaps pain from having known the memory of an ancestor's glory without being able to recreate it in his own skin, which now seemed to him to be deteriorating, yellowish, like that of the dead. What he wanted from me, I suspected, was to attempt to drain my essence from me to him; I don't know how...my resistance is worthy of a god. And I would resist even more strongly with his greed on top of me. Everything that happened to me would be advantageous, and I'd become invincible. In this improvised visit, I tried not to look at the young Englishman in his dark civilian suit. Yes, he could destabilize my moment of silent victory, unlike the old gentleman, who no longer had any kind of human fortune to battle my maniacal perseverance. So I stared at the old man. I began to wish for the meeting to end. If I stared at him

LORD

hard enough, like a daring lover asking for everything or nothing, he would no longer be able to find what was in his pockets, his past would rise with all its mold, his spirit would tremble more than his hands; if I kept my gaze steady, staring back at him, he would bow his head, as he in fact did. And then he withdrew.

We left the house and went down the deserted street. I felt the albino maid throwing a last glance after our slow steps. We turned onto Great College Street and walked through an archway leading to a vast courtyard surrounded by beautiful, ancient buildings—one of them was an alternative entrance to Westminster Abbey. There, the schools were as old as the buildings. Teenagers in suits and ties were playing with a soccer ball on the lawn and using terrible curse words. The ball landed at my English companion's feet. He kicked the ball and got into the game with the kids. He kept the ball near his feet until the boys came at him in a solid block and stopped him from using his arms. They took him down, shouting vile obscenities at this man twice their age, now a hindrance to their game. In a matter

of seconds, there were several teenagers on top of
my companion's body in a mix of anger and joking.
Then they suddenly backed off. There he was, his
suit all muddy, his face dirty, his hair disheveled.
And he smiled. He looked at the blue sky and
smiled, absorbed in that hiding place of the old
British aristocracy, a neighbor of Westminster. No
one passed; it was a rather semi-private place... Just
the tie-clad gang of students, and he, who was now
standing up and cleaning himself off. And I—a
stranger who had once been invited to participate...
in what? The boys gave up their game and dis-
persed...and my companion on our walk continued
to trot ahead, finding a way out that led us right to
the front entrance of the Abbey. We looked at each
other. Then I remembered that I hadn't looked at
myself in a mirror in a long time. What was he staring at? *Forget it*, I said to myself. It's only a man with
no external qualifications but the congenital idiocy
to take the initiative to leave this place, to try his
luck someplace else, preferably in the English countryside; to turn into an animal, to eat with his hands,
to cause fear, to sleep before people even begin

having dinner or arranging their parties, to wake up in the dark and let out a loud fucking scream, to throw himself from a rock, to bruise himself all over, to thus languish for days, and not survive the first blooming—turning as blue as the flowers until he blends in with everything and nobody notices him anymore. We had already walked a little way and now we stood looking at each other in front of Parliament, with people passing by all around us. We had to decide: Nothing was right; it was no use for him to keep me under house arrest in Hackney again. If he would at least tell me what he really wanted from me, I would try, I swear. If the council that governed him came to me and asked me to do the worst…who knows, I would do it, yes, I would, even if it implied my death. I would die happy in London, I swear. What I couldn't do was go back to Brazil. I would even kill to keep that from happening. I was baring my cowardice, I swear. My hands were free, waiting for the gun. I didn't give a shit about the consequences. Or did they think a man couldn't snap out of being a coward? It's not just a snap, man: it's being stuck in this limbo between staying in England and going back to South America that made me unrecognizable to myself anymore, it didn't let me transfigure myself, it wouldn't let me leave this stupid little body here, vomit myself out in disgust, or turn me into someone else. He was looking at me in front of Parliament. He looked like he had never seen me before. He was in danger, too. He had failed, man, he had failed—I wasn't the guy. Is there any other conclusion to come to? And was he who they thought he was? And that's why he was staring at me in front of the British Parliament now, in the middle of that crowd of tourists. Our instants coincided, finally. We were two men who now had found themselves on a seriously wrong path. Was there any way to get out of this mess painlessly? For me, maybe, I might be able to, with less pain than him. Well, everything had conspired to bring me to a new country. Why not another new city, another new region now? Could anything possibly cause me more pain? Could things get even worse? I sighed in relief. He understood. Understood everything. He understood that the condemned man here was not me. But I also understood that he wouldn't make things any easier for me. That the case was not over for him yet. He'd do anything to reinvent the potential he had seen in me, which I had always been unaware of. I saw in his sharp eyes, as if they lassoed me, that nothing else but me interested him. I wondered if our roles couldn't be reversed; if I could become his master. I looked up at Big Ben high above, its bells ringing, and realized that this reversal was impossible from where we stood. I could continue my stay in England, which would be the only way for me to continue carrying on with what I still had left, but I had to get away from this little shit of an Englishman, and fast. I had almost done it before, managing to take the train as far as Hither Green—still a London suburb—when I first thought of running away, hadn't I? How far would I be able to get this time? I mean, to leave it all behind: to get out of the train station; to see the village; to stay in a little hotel with the rest of the money from the "grant" that the little Englishman had given me; to meet an Englishwoman from the region; to nest with her; to take her children, if she had them, to the nearest amusement park; to run and rejoice; and this time, to really transform myself into a good-looking Latin man working at a cafe, a man completely trusted by the boss until one day he leaves everything to me and returns without heirs to Italy while his business prospers here. So, what do we do now? I ask the Englishman in front of Big Ben. The Englishman is speechless. He has contracted the same disease as the old man, the neighbor of T. E. Lawrence whom he took me to visit earlier that day. They are all mute. The moon appears behind him. A full moon. He's lit up in the moonlight. Mute. Hardened. He's made of stone, he's made of bronze, like the many statues of heroes that populate this city. Rush hour has passed. Few people are around. The moon has changed position but still illuminates him. He remains the same: all hardness and silence. He seems to want to say that from now on it will be like this: he'll just be an inspiration for those who accept him as bigger than he is—the specter of his success, an apparition. A few policemen circled around us, that's for sure. I walked away, crossing the street; I was quick, it's always good to remember that one is Brazilian at times like these. When I reached the other side, I turned. He was still standing there, near the Parliament gates, a police officer approaching. Suddenly he begins to walk, he sees me, yards away, and comes toward me, whistling. He's become someone else—sweet like I've never seen him. He seems to have forgotten that he's in trouble, that he chose the wrong guy for whatever part he had envisioned for me. But he won't give me his arm to twist so easily; he'll resume the plan and finally say what he had wanted, but only up to where it doesn't undermine his power. Now he will say what he thinks a true Englishman should be: an illusionist of propriety. Is that it? I want to ask him, but before I do an idea comes to me: I should take advantage of this chivalrous situation with the little Englishman until the end, until he pays me another subsistence installment, as he likes to call it. We walk along the edge of the Thames, sitting sometimes on benches that are high up so we can better appreciate the landscape. He no longer looks like one of the city's uncontested guardians. It seems like he's following me this time. He appears to have lost his way, to not know where he is. We sit on one of the elevated benches. I take his hand. I say: This is the Thames. Look at the moon over there. I take his hand in mine and kiss it. I'm suspicious of his reserved kindness. In a little while he'll lose control and show me again who's really in charge here. I unlock my hand from his and put it on his leg, patting his thigh. And I move to the edge of the bench. I begin to suspect that this man has lost the mortar that kept him so hard, strange, and oblique. Maybe he has fallen in love with me, that's all, and now he just wants to be with me. Maybe he's the one man for me and has simply arrived late in the game, when I don't even want to look at myself in the mirror anymore. This is happening on the banks of the Thames, under bright fucking moonlight. Who could say no? Is there anyone out there emotionally repressed enough to suggest that a pair of enraptured fags on the banks of the Thames is something laughable? Well, look, I'm going to take his hand again and he won't say anything; he'll just close his eyes and accept it. But, of course, I don't do any of this—I don't want to lose the reluctance that should exist in cases such as this.

Reluctance on both sides, understand? Here and there. And of course, it's London and begins to drizzle. And like two good Londoners, we don't speak of getting out of the dampness to stay dry. I take his hand again, and…no reaction again. But I don't overdo it. I return his sweet hand to his leg that's covered by his impeccable, marine cut trousers. I pat it twice. And I stop bothering him. The day breaks. And people show up in their rush-rush. Traffic everywhere. I ask him if he remembers that today is payday, as was stated in the invitation letter. I tell him I have an envelope in my pocket full of receipts to give to him. His answers are more decisive now. Ah…he's waking up. Is it today? Yes it is, I answer.

He gets up. He turns out his completely empty pants pockets. And he starts to walk with his feet pointed out, as in some silent movie comedy bit. I don't know what I'm supposed to feel faced by this figure. He keeps going with that pathetic walk, making people turn to look. He keeps going, his obdurate parsimony has no logic, his antics are more extreme than of any other English person. He keeps

JOÃO GILBERTO NOLL

going, like a clown, a drunk, a madman. As if the
pockets of his seemingly impeccable suit have holes
in them. I start going after him. I keep a bit of distance so no one suspects any connection between us.
We walk along the bank of the Thames and the
wind is freezing. I see a heap at the foot of a bench.
I don't know why the thing catches my eye so
strongly that it pulls me over to see what it is. A
piece of cloth. I open it. I feel it in my hands—a
cloth full of patches and stitchings, studded with
buttons here and there. A quilt—no, a cloak. Yes,
there is a gold button to close it at the base of the
neck. Did someone throw a theatrical costume in
the trash? I wrapped myself in the cloak. It smelled
like a chest of drawers…just that. I put my hands to
my chest; I looked at the river and I pretended that
it was actually just a branch of a small creek. I remembered the little Englishman behind me, and
suddenly he was stumbling toward the new pedes-
trian bridge over the Thames. It was suspended by
white bars. There are two, by the way: the Golden
Jubilee Bridges. I quicken my step. He doesn't look
back once. He's no longer imitating the silent movie

walk. I am literally shuffling, but I need to keep moving. I draw near. I take off the cloak and put it around his shoulders. I button it. The golden button was clearly made by a first-rate craftsman. I tell him: Go, you are the king, the sovereign, the bishop. He climbs up onto the first of the bridges, scales it and goes. The day is gone in the blink of an eye. It's night again. There's nobody close by. I applaud, shout loudly, and salute him. But then I stop…a sign that I can't go beyond this rite of passage. I don't know if he's still listening to me, but he stops in the middle of the bridge, as if he's just remembered something. Remembered what? He climbs onto the bridge's white iron structure then throws himself over. I will never forget the noise he made upon impact. It was not a noise meant for the world to hear. It was profound, cavernous; and as quickly as it came, it went. I was struck by the speed with which the day had passed by, this day in which we both inhabited the very same space, between that bench on the stone platform and this bridge. When someone kills themselves in public, even if it's dawn and there's no one around, the curious always seem to appear, as if out of nowhere. More and more people gathered. That's what happened. I stayed close. Those who had been taking in the scene from afar came snooping; they were the first witnesses: and they saw that yes, it had been a suicide. So I stayed close by; I had nothing to fear. A helicopter followed, firefighters. Ropes were unfurled from above. It was already day again. And now his body emerged from the water, tied with a rope, without the king's cloak. No shirt or jacket. Just his pants. His back was very white. It had the tone of wax as it hovered above the Thames. The right hand was injured. One foot was bare. The foot appeared to be the most alive area of his body: the bluish veins still seemed to want to keep going for some decisive moment when they would spread and reach farther than that little body and finally blend with the sky. I couldn't hear what anyone was saying. I just kept thinking: and now, what will I do now? And he didn't even pay me what he owed me. The first thing that came to mind was once again the thought of escaping into the English country-side, not drawing attention to myself, and continu-ing to avoid mirrors. If they come to speak with me,

I'll answer, but I'll only say what is necessary for my survival—I know…I'm not great at conversing, since all I know is how to write books, you know? I looked at my hands as the police covered the body. They were also pale, from playing the piano too much in my childhood and adolescence. I was lucky, I never left the scene of the death, but no police officer had come to talk to me as a potential witness. Me? Witness to what? I witnessed the cloak he preferred to leave behind: the cloth that was now rising to the water's surface, which no one would ever connect to the suicide. Were they related? I didn't even know, so large had been the laconic combustion of the last hours. I smiled widely at the river's gray waters: I was a survivor in bloom. As the police van drove past with its deafening siren, clearing the way, I looked at the golden friezes on the towers of Parliament and felt like I was some responsible underling. Another glance at the river, which was carrying the cloak away at such a speed that it was almost out of my sight now. Soon it would be evening again and so on and so on, and maybe I had no choice in my destiny; I didn't need details about where in England I needed to go, and what to do there... Perhaps, I might simply let myself be carried away, and thus manage to live for many years with some relative semblance of health...nothing too grim, maybe even interesting at times. So let me keep standing here on the edge of the Thames—or no, not that at all, for I was in danger of following the path of the Englishman who had invited me to London; there were plenty of reasons for this guy here to follow in the steps of his old boss. So I left the wall by the river. I farted. I needed to shit, take a good piss. Direction? The National Gallery, since they have good bathrooms there, you can dry your hands well with hot air. And as a bonus I could take a good look at Cézanne's bathers, I could get cozy in the museum's warmth, watching the Dutch, Caribbean, and Japanese paintings pass before my eyes. Time almost seems to be saying: Stay a while, don't go yet. That's what I was thinking as I sat on a toilet in the basement of the National Gallery. I pulled up my pants, which hadn't been washed for more than a month, and asked myself: Should I go stand in front of the bathers? Or Van Gogh's sunflowers? As I dried my hands under the hot air, I noticed a guy looking at me in a way that was more suggestive than one might expect from a decent gentleman. I looked at him, too. I winked. And I could have kept flirting with him, but another more urgent matter occurred to me. I was beginning to think that the guy who had stayed in bed at Bloomsbury Hospital had finally returned, that he had been reborn back inside me. But no, I didn't want to look at myself in the mirror—this was not something to be played around with. The bathroom was empty again. People stare, smile, flirt, but when push comes to shove, they don't want to kiss, they don't want to fool around. Climbing up the stairs to the ground level, the guy turned around, looking at me as if he wanted to do stuff. Then I was the one who didn't want to; I was so tired from the very recent death in the family, which had happened in such a devastating manner. I shook my head, and the man certainly thought my nod was an act of condescension to his willing gaze; and he laughed until I heard the tone of his laughter. But I didn't want any of that. I wanted to sit in front of the bathers—I hoped the bench was still vacant so it would be all mine—and wait for the museum to close so the painting would also rest, get some sleep. I woke up with a museum guard whispering to me, Sir, sir; Yes, I replied, straightening my crumpled coat. The arm I had been using as a pillow to support my body was completely numb. The guard wouldn't take his eyes off me. Detail: I was not sitting in front of Cezanne's bathers or Van Gogh's sunflowers; random luck had brought me to choose a vase of flowers by Gauguin as my painting to contemplate. Indeed, Gauguin's vase was the most beautiful painting of the three. The guard kept staring at me. The museum was closing...before descending the stairs outside the museum, I still had time to see Trafalgar Square framed by the museum's columns. I moved between different pairs of columns; I leaned on the railing, and admired new framings of the square in the darkening afternoon. Once again, I had needed time to decide. I went down the stairs thinking that I wouldn't go back to my dungeon in Hackney. I was a prisoner of nothing but time, and time urged me on, as always. I had

to kill it, time. I had to kill it by walking around
until I decided what train to take, what English
town to go to, or even if I should rest in a little hotel
still in London, but as far away from Hackney as
possible. Doves, doves were closing in on me. Suddenly they descended and I needed to protect myself
as if facing a catastrophe. Everything is a matter for
consideration when deep down what you're trying
to do is to postpone some thorny decision. Here are
doves, there is a beautiful woman trying to guess my
nationality, farther ahead a tourist surrounded by
suitcases, involved in the process of boarding his
special bus. A police siren. The city's hasty drizzle.
All deserve extreme attention when you're treading
water. I put my hands in my pockets. I see I still have
cash for a coffee or two, maybe a little something
more. Who knows if the Englishman had a few
pounds in the jacket he discarded in the confusion
of his death, gifting the money to the Thames. That
asshole only showed me his pants pockets. I went
into a porn store. About seven, eight men in a tight
room surrounded by videos with covers such as one
white cock entering a cunt while a black cock is

already in the ass. I looked at the clock as if I had to be somewhere and left. At Charing Cross, an old man looked at me intently. Why not sleep in one of these cheap hotels with this old man and spend a night lying in bed thinking for a few more hours? He'll pay, of course—I'll be very clear from the start. This many pounds. You want to? That way I could, perhaps, buy a train ticket. I stopped in front of a store, pretending to admire some postcards of London. The old man stopped at the edge of the sidewalk. He turned slowly, looking at me. Was he English? No, he was an Indian man, and had some money in his pocket. Dark skin. Hair still black. Small body. Good health. Maybe I could even save some money. Spend a month fucking the old man, serving the old man. Then I'd figure out where to go, what to do regarding my painful situation. I grabbed a postcard of Piccadilly Circus, or whatever, and my anxiety was such that I tore it—up and down, right to left. I shredded it all to pieces. The Turkish owner of the gift store said he was going to call the police. I said he didn't need to, and gave him my coins. Then I started walking in the opposite direction of the old Indian man. However, he stayed on my mind, but as something that didn't translate exactly into sex anymore, but just as a meager piece of flesh that could at least support me: from a tiny olive pit on the sidewalk seemed to emanate the true compassion I had lost somewhere, I don't even know where anymore. I was a man without compassion and he, this small old man, would teach me how to have it again. My daily, carnal contact with him—I repeat, with a man who was as tiny as a flower— would temporarily restore my physicality, like bankrupt tenants still occupying their home. But the old man, oh: he could even pay me for my already worn-out body. What he was doing on the curb was calling me to join the occult practices of old age, when two people can, at last, pay the long-overdue debts of their bodies and soul. Someone next to me asked me the time and I jumped, scared; I thought it was the old man and that I'd have to actually go with him. I looked back, imagining he was following me. But I had lost the old man in the crowd. So I had to keep on going alone—which was already my addiction; I was like someone who doesn't realize he has

an addiction because it has become his natural state.
To have someone next to me all the time, someone
to talk to, to express opinions to, to discuss the landscape with, notice the events around us, and the distant ones too, to sacrifice emotionally in order to
save the relationship, all of this represented a sacrifice, not of myself, but of the perspective that had
taken me over completely, and maybe I won't get
even more lost. What perspective could be so zeal-
ous, so self-absorbed? That's when I stopped at the
corner, took off my cap, and summoned the devil. I
called the evil thing two, three times, to come rescue
me. Then I stepped back and leaned against the
building. I held the cap upside down in the air, as if
to ask for a few cents from the passing crowds of
young people. If someone looked at me, I'd disguise
myself and shake my cap. No one was watching me.
I'd get into position to beg again, beg for help. In the
blink of an eye I could be anyone. It was bewildering
to me; it made me go into a sort of trance of heat
and night sweats, I fell into vertigo, a cloud took me
away. I managed to keep holding on to people's
woolen sleeves; I sat down on a step. They asked me

how I felt—voices, many voices. I begged for for-giveness; unfortunately, only for forgiveness. Sud-denly, I had become a saint, feeling that my body looked like a blasphemy in Charing Cross, disturbing the rushing pedestrians by its mere pres-ence. I looked at the variety of faces trying to help, and the deepest regret descended upon me. What have I done? I was the one asking. And they all re-sponded, almost in unison, nothing, nothing, you're good. The more I tried to console myself, lying on that corner, the more the city opened up my abscess. I asked myself, silently, if I'd be able to survive the night. Would London know how to finish me…? Or not…? And I decided to keep going. I got up, unrolled the sleeves of my shirt, quickly put on my jacket, and walked away, asking not to be bothered anymore… I'd had enough. I looked through the glazed windows, at what was inside the cafes. I looked…I looked so much that I wished I could blind myself for a few hours, lie in bed, under the blankets, without worrying if sleep or whatever would come; it was like a desire to masturbate, any-thing that would distract me for at least a second from my solitary obsession to see, okay, to see the distance I still had to go, willingly or not. I swore I would leave that bed knowing, step by step, what I had to do on this holy day. At least on that holy day I would not be walking as I was now through Charing Cross, thinking about the restorative power of a bed and a blanket and the blessed blindness available between these two elements. Hold me! I want to ask a stranger passing by. Hold me! Because I'm going to fall and never rise again. Hold me! Ma'am, hold me, you brat, because this man you see here is going to levitate, hover, fly over the city until he lands at a train station that will take him away. That will take me…where? Where will they welcome me as the prince that I deserve to be? I went into one of those large London bookstores, which are everywhere, and I searched for translations of my books. I found them. What do they mean, if I don't even know where to go now, where to sleep, what money I would use to eat and survive? In those intervals I didn't give a damn about writing a single line, what work was I doing? Incidentally, from now on, what work will I do, since my indifference to the written word becomes clearer each day? Sweep…to sweep cafes was the answer. To fight with specks of dust that don't want to leave their corners. To find my way with a broom until the dust finally comes off the floor and I get a little relief from having to curse at things. To fight earnestly with the dust, and to have a bed to sleep in, in some rented room. A newspaper whose content lasts a week. To set aside change for next week's paper. I was in the bookstore, holding two copies of my own books, and wondering if the solution really was to leave London. Dust, bed, newspaper—none of that was lacking here. Whom to ask? If I spent a sleepless night walking through the city, I would have the answer by the next morning; it would come as if it had slipped from my own mouth…

So that's what I did. I changed direction. I turned back toward Trafalgar Square. But I'd be lying if I said I walked back through those places I had just passed. I was as alone as a man wandering in a sprawling forest, comprised of nothing but trees and the sounds of nocturnal animals. Sometimes I would squat and pick up chunks of dried leaves from the damp soil. They were so mulched into the ground that they affixed themselves to me with the glue of earth, without any effort, to my face and neck. I was camouflaged, so they wouldn't recognize me, they, the ones who had given orders to the little Englishman who had just jumped off the bridge, discoloring himself even more—forever in the waters of the Thames. I had witnessed his floating body hanging from ropes, swinging over the city, and his skin had had a quick and devilish necrosis— it was covered with a whiteness unrelated to any mortal's pigmentation. White like a blessed cloud or a virgin's sheet. He could have been my saint that night with all that whiteness of his. I covered my skin with more and more leaves in that place that should still be Charing Cross or at least close by. I walked a little more. I saw a sudden flash. I stopped. Ah, a girl was taking pictures of an actor dressed in vintage clothes, sitting in the backstage doorway of a large London theater. It might have been between scenes and he was resting. I shook the leaves off and approached him. Please, I said, just a minute: I'm a journalist and I want to do a quick interview with you. I don't have more than a five-minute break, he said. He believed me; he was paying attention. I don't need more time than that. What's your role? An eighteenth-century man who hopes to be reincarnated as his sister. He, this man I play, confesses his eagerness, but is taunted in the tavern. One day he steals his sister's clothes and goes into the ladies' room while wearing them. He joins a convent. The nuns all run away. He cuts off his sexual organs with a dagger and offers them to the goddess Maria. Goddess…that's how the piece treats her. It's by an author from Madrid. I tell him right away that none of that interests me. The girl continues with the photographs because the guy is handsome. The fact that I had said I was a journalist and what he had told me didn't interest me, didn't seem to disillusion him or even upset him. He rehearses a smile in a final pose for the girl. Tell me something, I ask him. I'm just thinking…what do you think of me going to live in Liverpool? It's my hometown, I came from there, he responds a little enthusiastically. If you go, don't hesitate to reach out to my mother. I'll go back one day too, you'll see. Yes, I'll see, I answer. I burst out laughing as he goes back into the theater through the dark backstage. I try to look inside, but someone comes and closes the door. The girl with the camera laughs a lot too, joining me. People circle around us—the joyful couple in the streets of London. At the end of it I grieve ferociously, speaking through the door that is closed in my face: What about your mother's address in Liverpool? How about the addresses of all the mothers in this country? Then I began to prowl, sometimes desperately, in search of a salvation from someone affectionate and kind, which had taken on the figure of the actor from Liverpool in that moment and who burned his own genitals as an offering to, according to the playwright from Madrid, that goddess above all other goddesses, Maria. I grew taciturn as if I deeply pondered the disgrace in where I might go, to some corner somewhere, to be lost to starvation or whatever... But I'll never stop; if London wanted to expel me, then now was the time for that ritual—I would only stop to learn what station the train to Liverpool arrived at, and in fact, I stopped to ask a young Englishman. He had a face of someone from the countryside who finds themselves now in a post-punk stage, something like that, and the boy knew, as I had imagined, where to catch the train to Liverpool, having just come from there. I swear, he grew enthusiastic as he talked about the city, another sign that it was where I should go—and so I would! The train left from Euston Station. I needed to go through the Bloomsbury neighborhood, past Russell Square, and keep going on, always. No way to go wrong. I got it, kissed the English boy's hand, thanked him, and went. Even if I had to cross desert and mountains I would get there; I would get to Euston Station, take a train, and in three hours, as the English boy had told me, I'd arrive—with my hands not in my pockets, letting them feel the pain of the icy wind that comes from the city's piers, and waiting for the best to come my way. On a corner in Bloomsbury, a totally unexpected need to vomit hit me. I wiped myself with a sheet of newspaper that was fluttering by. But I couldn't stop; I realized it was London I was throwing up, London with its ghosts and impossible missions, already entirely unsuccessful. Now, alternatively, I was not going to try anything in Liverpool, the conditions would draw me in by their own genius, nothing else. I stopped again for a little bit to see if any more spew would come from my mouth; I felt the onset of nausea… Hands to my chest, numb. But nothing came out, so I continued like lightning to Euston Station.

I arrived at the great hall and sat down. Many people were standing, looking up at departure times and platforms listed on the brightly lit elevated displays. I shivered as I realized that the trip to Liverpool was really happening. The train left at seven in the morning. I was surprised that it was already five-thirty. I looked outside: true, it was getting light. Time seemed to speed up to win me over. I had just spoken with the actor who castrates himself on stage each night, and now, suddenly, it's dawn. I decided that in Liverpool, I would become a Spartan warrior, exercising every morning and timing each movement. I wouldn't let myself get distracted. I'd get in sync. The entirety of the movement and its necessary duration. I would try to master time, make a friendly arrangement with the day, from the moment I awoke until the moment I

fell asleep, thus allowing sleep to serve as the time
of my independence, until one day it would come
to stay forever. This idea made my left foot shake.
As I bent to rub the foot and soothe it, I felt the
urge to rise—it was now or never, I could not wait
any longer. Many passengers were hurrying through
the station, and I chose one. I walked toward him.
I only had eyes for the chestnut velvet collar of his
unbuttoned brown overcoat. That velvet collar will
always be engraved in my mind. He was well off,
which is what I noticed immediately: I bumped into
him; in an instant I'd insinuated my forefinger and
thumb into his overcoat, into the top inside pocket
over his heart, right there, and I took his wallet and
put it into the hip pocket of my own coat, all in one
absurdly quick movement. I did it, giving all those
excuses the English use when bumping into someone, but I said it all so much more emphatically, because this was a collision provoked by someone like
me, who should never touch a gentleman. Ever.

I stood in the middle of the crowd, stock still
and trembling. Instead of leaving the scene of the
crime, I followed the velvet collar of the gentleman

JOÃO GILBERTO NOLL

whom I had just stolen a sum from out of the corner of my eye—I was still unaware of the exact sum.
Still standing there, I could see the man's chestnut
velvet collar as absolute proof that my subtraction
would mean nothing to him, even if it was too
much by my own standards—and that was the hope
I cultivated as I stood there for a while longer, as if
delaying the pleasure of knowing the amount and
incorporating it once and for all into my financial
vocabulary. Let's hope! I shivered in the cold. The
notes of a nocturne came to my mind, played by a
fine pianist, and still hearing its evasive cadence I
went looking for a restroom. I found it and entered
a stall. I pulled out the wallet, opened it: it held
all the money I would need for a long time. New
pound notes, as if they had been freshly withdrawn
from the bank. That man was lucky. I was luckier.
The stall smelled bad and all, but to be there: away
from the camera's eye, worshipping the new life I
could now have for a while, counting and recount-
ing the bills that were so fresh from the mint that
they crackled as they became my property... Ah,
that feeling negated any fetidness I smelled—any

imperfection, disaffection, or incomprehension.

I was careful to keep my promise and not look in the mirror while I washed my hands. If I looked at myself in the mirror, I'd be breaking the spell I had cast with such grace at Euston Station. I asked for a seat on the next train to Liverpool. Preferably next to the window so I could admire the famous English fields. The fat clerk didn't like my requests and gave me a blank stare. But having the ticket in my hand was what really mattered. What really mattered was to liberate myself from that secretive situation in London. And to be able to go, to go wherever, and leave everything behind, even if my everything was little more than nothing. To let go of fear, even if my fear of being persecuted by a shadow power in the city only existed in my head. With ticket in hand, I stood in front of the brightly lit displays where so many others also stood as if in some pre-trip ritual, and I saw that the train to Liverpool departed from platform 7. I hurried. I still believed there would be a plainclothes officer at the door of my car ready to ask for my papers and then interrogate me in a room at the station. I got on the train

like any other passenger. It was cozily warm inside. I
was not going to see any English countryside, no sir,
what I needed was to curl up and fall deeply asleep.
I woke up to a female voice announcing Liverpool
station. It was a bright morning, unlike any I had
seen in London. A sky so clear…without a single
cloud. Ah, but even though it was the end of winter,
it was still very cold. It was windy with the force of a
port city—a river, and also the sea. Out on the sidewalk, my cap was constantly blowing off of my head
in the wind. I clung to the walls, sometimes afraid
of being dragged away in a real typhoon. Until I
came across a grand hotel. It was similar to Hotel
Gloria in Rio. It was called the Britannia Adelphi
Hotel. The Adelphi, I later learned, was what they
called it locally. I was told it had hosted kings and
queens. That on the Beatles' first return to their
hometown, now universally acclaimed, they stayed
at the Adelphi and waved to the crowd from the
hotel's grandest window. I didn't know any of that at
the time. I was leaning against the wall of a nearby
building, and all I saw was a fortress, safe enough to
shelter me from typhoons, at least for my first few

days there. I went into my room and it was all true. It had a big bed with a satin quilt that I rolled on as soon as I saw it. Just one problem: too many mirrors. I grabbed sheets and pillowcases, and with my eyes closed like a child playing alone, I covered them up, so they would not tempt me to the point where I would no longer be able to resist. But I didn't forget to wash my face thoroughly before I went out into the city for the first time. Just passing through the lobby was a feast of gilded friezes and chandeliers. I was staying in a palace and I had the money to afford it for a few days. I hadn't forgotten to ask for a map of Liverpool at the front desk. I ordered ravioli Bolognese from a red-headed boy at a restaurant on the corner. I asked him where the Cavern was, the first place, according to legend, the Beatles had performed. He asked me if I had a map. I opened it up on the table. He immediately found the spot and made a little circle around the famous pub, not far from there. I began to notice that many people on the street were wearing green T-shirts and hats. And that the pubs had live bands playing old Irish songs as the crowds sang along. In that hell of cold wind, girls wore miniskirts and T-shirts with their sleeves rolled up to the shoulders, and the guys didn't have coats on, several of them even wore shorts. They were all dancing like people did during Carnival in Brazil, but with a lasciviousness that outdid even the revelers in Rio. I asked around—oh yes, it was March 17—Saint Patrick's Day, the patron saint of Ireland—which was the reason for all the parties and the sounds of Irish music imprinted upon the city. But I drifted away from the loudest pubs, drifted away from the most animated crowds on the sidewalks, drifted away until I found the Cavern. I went down three floors. It was indeed a cave. It was impossible to believe that four boys were able to fit on what they called a stage that looked like it could barely fit two. It was dark; only two or three tourists. Is it really here? I asked the waiter. It is… Do you want a beer? I do, I answered. Then I remembered that I hadn't put alcohol in my mouth for nine years. I sat at a table at the bottom of the tilted floor in front of the stage in pitch darkness. Only the bar and the stage were dimly lit. The beer came. I drank it all at once. A bit of alcohol seemed necessary to withstand the typical harbor winds of the English north. And some drinking buddy would know when to put his hand on my arm to make me stop. Looking at the stage, I didn't see the Beatles, but myself with a face I no longer expected to have. A marble statue, the head tilted to the side, grossly disproportionate—Me! If it were still possible to remember my real past. The head occupied almost the entire stage and I drank, hidden in the dark in front of it. A sort of shame was making me die a little in the dark. I couldn't die too much, because there was Liverpool and the new life it promised. I would not let go of that, whether I liked the city or not. I was going to go out to buy clothes now, basic necessities: soap, toothpaste, scissors, whatever. No hidden dissidents from any English institution would catch me here. I would begin again, do everything over from the start; I would depend exclusively on my own skills, of which I would blow at every dormant ember.

I bought some stuff I needed. I got in lines at mini-marts, I felt at home thanking the clerks for the change. Everything had the neat smell of being itself: the cleaning products, personal hygiene items, fruits, vegetables. Everything seemed ready and waiting for me. As I thanked the owner of an establishment, I looked at the other people in line: good humor reigned. On my way back to the hotel, I saw long lines of young people in summer clothes waiting to enter the pubs. The security guards, usually black, mostly wore black jackets and tried to keep order at the entrances to these parties. The young people walked in groups, shouting words that I no longer understood properly because they were so drunk. Even though the calendar verified we were living in the agony of winter, the sun was shining in the late afternoon. Spring was announcing itself, that was it, buds were ready to burst on a few trees. Even though parts of the city were ugly, decayed in fact, everything came to me as dawning beauty, and with a barbarous, primitive air; a particular beauty that was hidden from the eyes of the tourists— nourishing itself from an era when Europe hadn't yet become a myth. I felt so grateful that I hugged the groceries instead of holding the bags by their handles. I even came to a halt and wondered if life after death couldn't be possible. I thought of non-sense like that. I walked into the Adelphi feeling at home. I put the groceries on the bed and looked out the window. How was it possible I hadn't looked out here before? I wondered. Then the phone in the room rang. Who could it be in a city where I didn't know anyone? A professor at the University of Liverpool, who spoke Portuguese with a European accent, wanted to see me. I found it funny that she said the name of the local university in Portuguese: *Universidade da Cidade de Liverpool*. She was wait-ing for me in the lobby. I made a move to go to the mirror and remove the cloth that covered it—more than anything to just check myself out. But I resisted the temptation. Then I went downstairs. And when the elevator door opened on the ground floor, a porter stood in front of me and said, She's the one waiting for you. The professor was a young woman, in her thirties, if that. She seemed cautious. She said she had seen me on the street and recog-nized me as the author she used to read and study with her students. She'd decided to enter the hotel and ask if I was indeed a guest. And she didn't want to wait—she asked them to call me. For a specific reason: they were in urgent need of a Portuguese teacher—not of literature, she stressed, but of the Portuguese language—for next semester. And when she saw me going into the hotel she asked herself: Who's a better master of Portuguese than a writer of so many books in the language? I could leave all the practical stuff to her, the papers and everything else I'd need from Brazil. I quietly responded that I could give it a try, since, in my head, I spoke Portuguese all the time. Gradually, I began to get excited and cite numerous grammarians who came to mind, pondering their theses on various aspects of the Portuguese language—until I took a deep breath and fell into an armchair in the lobby. I will apply for the position, I said firmly. And she replied that I was the man, there was no other. I remembered that I had begun my life as a Portuguese teacher, and that syntax was my favorite area. At last I sighed, beaten into submission by the good winds that had brought me an invitation from this young Englishwoman.

The next morning I put on my new coat and

went up the hill to the university campus, near the hotel. The Englishwoman introduced me to the head of the department, a Portuguese professor, bald, in his sixties, a specialist in medieval Iberian studies. He could speak for hours about the *Larvos*, a group of wanderers who swept across the region in the twelfth century announcing the forgiveness that had not previously been granted for man's eagerness in charging his steed against nature. We went out to talk, walking around the cold, overcast, terribly foggy campus. Both of us had our hands held behind our backs. I played with the idea of comparing myself to the Larvos; me, who had left one decaying port in southern Brazil for another—in almost identical condition—in the northwest of England, so I could at last, on the cusp of old age, establish a home, make myself a cocoon with a fireplace, and tie the aforementioned steed to the same favorite tree forever. Along the paths, we laughed comfortably, and right then I felt already that I'd indeed be the one chosen to occupy a chair in the Portuguese Department at the University of Liverpool. Of course, I was not interested in literary theories, the exegeses, the metaphors, the palpitations in the souls of great writers. I was more interested in knowledge of the Portuguese language, how it had formed and with what face and dynamics it was presented today. Why we linked one word to another assembling phrases that were either sumptuous or dry, sinuous or direct, crude or subliminal. If what we said with such phrases had an immediate connection to real things or if it only served as a type of discharge from our incomprehensible neurons. And if this last hypothesis prevails, why don't we just shut up, even if that act would cause me to lose my job as a teacher of the delirium called the Portuguese language? We could then form a new department at the university, one for the canons of Silence; yes, with a capital *S* indeed, and in this department we could evoke what we have forgotten to expose and echo until now. In the beginning, it would be the only chair at the university, the new Theology, from which myriads of others and their many ramifications would emanate. I shook hands with the Portuguese professor and went down the hill, down to the pubs where I would find my future students binge drinking, where the stores called to me to buy more odds and ends to fill my room at the Adelphi. Should I put my hope in you? I asked the blowing wind. Should I wish to undo your enigma and embark upon finding your voice? Then I exploded into laughter with these supposedly age-old ruminations of mine, with which I entertained myself with nothing, or rather, with only the insignificant smiles of petty falsehoods. I— ready to become a Portuguese language teacher at a foreign university—was being overtaken by a thirst for nothingness. Then let me run to the pub, let me start drinking again, even if only a little, and let me undo, yes, my deal with the angels.

At the foot of the hill, very close to the Adelphi, I saw a pub with an ornate façade called the Beehive. I went in. It was already crowded. Did I even know what time it was? All I knew was that I was employed as a Portuguese professor, with students who mostly spoke English. This would be a good place to stay, since, free of my worries about London, I didn't want to leave the country anymore. It wasn't for nothing that I had attached myself to this island. I had been summoned by an indecipherable

Englishman from Brazil, that's not a lie, but he did not reveal the truth behind his actions or what he in fact represented until his last days, and the only thing I knew for certain were the initials of an institution that, in my view, was fraudulent. And that's all right, but I had to admit that the Englishman had somehow given me an opportunity to see what I needed: a new country, whether it was this one or another... But—since they had given me a plane ticket to come here, and this nation, so far, hadn't really rejected me to the point I felt the need to leave—look at where I was now: soon to be a tenured teacher at the University of Liverpool. Even if I had been crazy to exile myself from Brazil, I now had my cause: the Portuguese language to disseminate—don't forget, don't forget, I repeated, looking into my mug full of that very dark beer that makes a man who knows when to stop drinking it a true gentleman. Well...not quite yet...it's just the first beer, and I was standing—there wasn't a counter to lean against and The Beehive was a true hornet's nest of humans; I sweated endlessly. Then a man sitting alone at a table called me over. He was a bit

stocky, not as old as me, and he had called out to me.
As soon as I sat down I took off my new overcoat.
He had already cast off his coat, and wore a shirt
with the sleeves rolled up. I saw he had a tattoo on
his arm. A sun with many rays emanating from it.
He had been a deckhand on a cargo ship, but now,
with widespread unemployment at the port, he had
opened a small hardware store. He didn't want to
emigrate, as many of his colleagues at the docks
had. He lived in Liverpool, because he was born
and raised here and he liked it. He knew what to
do on Sundays and holidays. Those days, he didn't
open his shop, he went down to the sea instead. To
listen to seabirds. The seabirds I had heard on my
way here as I walked down the hill. I told him I was
being hired by the University of Liverpool to teach
Portuguese. Brazilian? he asked. Yes, I answered
emphatically, as if I wanted to start teaching immediately. Is Brazil as big as they say? Much bigger,
I answered. Are you going to miss it? No, I'm not.
And you think you'll like it here? If you teach me
how. And right there I noticed he was that drinking
buddy who would put his hand on my arm when I

had asked for one glass too many. The urgency in the environment was intense; it was necessary to speak many decibels above normal. I liked the guy and he liked me. There was a loneliness in him that could meet with mine…I don't know. It was mano a mano, no one could interfere with our already established fate. I ordered another beer, my second, but that was not what was making me so sure. The fact that he had a small business and I was a future Portuguese professor in the city and we had met in such a manner…everything had a way of coming together and nothing that was merely human could disrupt it. I had found my city, my home, my man, and even if I asked for a third glass of beer nothing would crumble. I said I was staying at the Adelphi for the time being. He laughed, laughed a lot, I don't know why he was laughing so much. Perhaps he was rebelling against the bourgeois condition. If he only knew that my lodging and everything had only been possible because of… I didn't know what he'd think. I didn't even want to know. All I know is that we ordered another beer and "La vie en rose" by Piaf was playing. And still tasting the last drink in our mouths, we went to the Adelphi. So he could see my room, its splendor without equal. Truly. *Ver-da-de*, I said in Portuguese, *pura verdade*.

The lights were on in the room. He lay down, said he'd had too much to drink. I lay on top of him, facing him, our faces so close that we couldn't recognize each other anymore. It was a mass of flesh in excess, which we only increased when we took off our clothes, never changing our positions—me on top of him, face to face. All of a sudden, we were naked. And just as suddenly, we had nothing to say. Then he settled under me, taking my cock in his hand and pressing it against his. He began to stroke them, slowly at first. I'd lift my hips to look. I covered his hand with mine, and he stroked us both at the same time. We were two men who—though no longer in the prime of our youths—still looked like two roosters, cockfighters at the peak of their strength, and who, instead of scuffling to the death, had entered into a new rite with the emission of fresh blood: this milk, that came out now in gushes, sullying our hands, bellies, groins, legs…

I woke up first, and found everything too white.

Like a photograph trying to accentuate the gray
tone coming through the window. I got up and tried
to see the city. It was impossible, either because of
the day's intense fog or simply because it was rain-
ing. The view from the window was completely dull.
There were faint shadows down the street. A United
Kingdom flag, which I had noticed before, now
only showed itself as an indistinct, floating stain. I
went to the next window: the same. I wondered if
the world would be like this from now on, foggy. If
there would be nothing solid left in it; if I should
not expect anything from it to be clearly defined;
if all I had allowed myself to aspire to in Liverpool
was disintegrating in this realm of imprecise forms,
where neither I nor anyone on this side had access to its history (spread throughout that empti-
ness in mere nuances of gray). I heard the shower.
I noticed there was a large cloud of steam coming
from the bathroom. I called softly, as if any voice
in here would be disturbing: George! No one answered. I called louder: George! Nothing. Then the
sound of the shower stopped. There was no noise at
all, not even coming from the street. And the vapor

dissipated, making the windows even foggier. I went to see. In the bathroom was no one. I had been cast off, left alone in a city that did not exist, was that it? Left confined to this room, with just a bathroom and a view of black-and-white spots, some gray or cream, mostly meaninglessness—would that be so bad? Portuguese classes, George—all buried within the chimera? What was left to do, I asked myself, to give passage to a new panorama, to unleash what was still trapped in my chest but maybe wanted to come out? I ripped the cloth off of the largest mirror in the room. In it, a whole person could be seen. But he too was blurred to obscurity. I wiped an area of the mirror with my hand, at the height of my face. It smeared, now even murkier. My fingers still carried traces of semen—mine and George's mixed together. The smear was right in front of my eyes, blocking my view. I picked up the sheet that had covered the mirror. I rubbed the glass, rubbed every corner, seeking out any small possibility of seeing my skin again.

The work was done. I went to turn on the lights so I wouldn't miss a thing… On the way, I noticed the door to the hallway was open. Had he run away? It didn't matter, his semen was still here, syrupy on my hand; it had to be someone else's, mine was not so dense, so gooey.

The first thing I saw in the mirror was a tattoo of the sun with emanating rays on my arm. I looked at the ground so I wouldn't be surprised by more. I murmured: But had that sun really been on my arm or on George's? The mirror confirmed the answer, and there was no use putting things off with more questions. Everything had been answered. I was not who I thought I was. George had not escaped, he was here.

There it was, only one man in the mirror: him.

Had someone escaped through the door? I propped it open; I needed to think... Did any off-shoot of myself still linger inside me, maybe enough to make him leave? And where else would someone go who had declared his desire to stay so clearly? Oh, no. I closed the door and turned the key.

Alone, I stared at my nakedness, my entire frame in the glass, surrounded by an ornate golden frame.

I am a Portuguese professor, I said in Portuguese, of course, eyes glued to the reflected image of that now lonely body, and with the mirror returning George's breath to me, which, contrarily, I breathed in: yes, into me, syllable by syllable... I am a Portuguese professor, I repeated in my Brazilian accent and with the same disposition, mine; except that—on another surface, more incisive, oily, with the thick mane of a barbarian—his. It was necessary to let the moment go, to try starting again, not to tell anyone. What if all of this came to nothing? Well, there was always the bed, open and generous, and I could always sleep on it and dream. George's dreams? I could travel through his evasive images, through those nocturnal sewers—I wanted to believe in this, hoping I could live some new adventures. Astute, I would absorb the matrix of the other's soul—but not the disagreeable ideas or the simple day-to-day sensations—with one intent: to store the essence of more life inside the chambers of my brain. Because, when the scoundrel gets lost in sleep, he passes his mind's rudder to a new giver, who fills his brains with his own script without a thread of filter: a fallen god, causing an outbreak.

And who would teach Portuguese? And the hardware store, would it close? Which of us would actually succeed in this story? Or would just one existence continue from the two? And what for? I almost revolted, without getting any specific response from this organism's nervous network. I wanted to lie down, to make George a living dead man and make him solve this thing for me. I would stay as long as my consciousness persisted and struggled, for this is the greatest task of our consciousness: to deny even in the midst of its desertion. It would be like this from now on. Or would it be just the opposite…?

Oh, come, George, come. I squeezed my new biceps on this arm, this same arm that came from my shoulder. Come, George, I repeated, without knowing if I was calling to someone, still disoriented by the act of translating myself from my own body. He had already transferred a solid physical autonomy to me. I had it. And I couldn't feel imprisoned in it. No: I rejoiced in this gain, smothering the gift in the bending of this abdomen, folding and stretching that leg, shaped by victorious soccer games in its puberty perhaps. Come, George, come…

I was driven by my own, brand new internal disorder. I pressed ahead: I got dressed and walked down the hall of the hotel with the determined steps of a new man. Outside, Liverpool was the same. Only now, it was bathed in sunlight. The streets enjoyed a fair sharpness. Kids ran around, caught up in laughter.

It was good to walk with a new muscular calibration. There was a little pain, unknown to me until then, in the lumbar. Upon thinking about it, it disappeared. My gestures widened, I grew.

I took a cab, asking to be taken to the oldest cemetery in town. The driver said he would take me to one, inactive since the nineteenth century; a few famous people were buried there. He didn't drive very far before he stopped in front of a graveyard. He asked if he should wait. I said no. And I walked among the rows. Seabirds screamed in the background, indiscernible. And I went beyond the last row into where a thicket had overtaken the place. All was still leafless, in the dryness of winter.

I jumped over a crumbling stone wall. I walked. I walked along, scraped by prickly branches, pushing them away. As if suddenly in an enchanted forest, on the eve of spring, I was going to have a place of my own. I took off my new coat and folded it several times. I lay on the dry grass, my head on my coat. I needed to fall asleep. See if I would dream the dream of the other, whose semen I swore I still had on my hand. It would be the irrefutable proof of what I would have to learn to accept... And I fell asleep...